Nuna Lake

Nuna Lake

A Story of Love Lost and Love Found

Helen Hendricks Friess

iUniverse, Inc.
New York   Bloomington

NUNA LAKE
A Story of Love Lost and Love Found

iUniverse books may be ordered through booksellers or by contacting:

iUniverse
1663 Liberty Drive
Bloomington, IN 47403
www.iuniverse.com
1-800-Authors (1-800-288-4677)

ISBN: 978-1-4401-4304-5 (pbk)
ISBN: 978-1-4401-4303-8 (ebk)

Printed in the United States of America

iUniverse rev. date: 6/2/2009

Chapter 1

"Goooood Morning, America! It's a beautiful day. And remember, this is the first day of the rest of your life."

The sound from the radio awakened Rosalind. She pulled her arm from under the covers and reached over to turn off the alarm. Her mind was instantly alert but her eyes and her body were a bit slower to wake up. As she cuddled back under the covers she remembered the date. It was a year ago today that her world had been turned upside down. It was a year ago tomorrow that she had really heard that same greeting as she woke up. Somehow she managed to hear the words *the rest of your life* very loud and strong each day this past year. Yes, she thought, for the past year I had to cling to that thought to even think there would be a rest of my life.

But I made it. And I'm doing OK. As she lay there in bed she remembered just how far she had come. She opened her eyes and could see the sunlight coming in the window; she could see the gauzy curtains blowing gently in the morning breeze. She could hear the chirping of the robins and finches as they staked out their territory. She smiled as she smelled the aroma from the hyacinths she had planted outside her window.

She knew that at times the aroma from them could be over-powering but she loved their bright vivid colors. As she had planted the bulbs last fall she was taking the first step toward a new life that spring brings and what's a better sign of spring than the early flowers swaying in the light breeze in all their glory. The daffodils were blooming and the early tulips were already in bud. Just like all that new life, she was determined to really make this the first day of the rest of her life.

She got out of bed, put on her robe and made her way to the kitchen. Thanks to the automatic timer (and remembering to set it the night before) her coffee was ready. She poured a big cup of coffee, stopped to pick up the morning paper from the front door and made her way to the swing on the big wraparound porch. This is a wonderful way to start the day she thought. Whoever thought I would be here today?

On this date a year ago, when the voice from the radio had awakened her, she hadn't heard the words about the rest of her life. She thought it was a routine day until she realized that Rob wasn't in bed. She usually arose first and was very surprised to find him in his suit ready to leave for work. He poured her a cup of coffee and told her to sit down. He had something to tell her. This would be the last morning he would be here. He was moving that very day to a new home with a new love of his life. It took all day for the words he said to really sink in - meeting his real love, his soul mate, a long time affair, a new job. Words like, this house is too big for you. Words like you can make it on your own. Words like you don't need me when he really meant I don't need you. As she heard his litany she realized that this was not a conversation, this was a speech; every word and every thought carefully planned out in advance. Every detail was in place. Everything arranged so there would be no need for changes in his plan. She sat there stunned, barely understanding that this wasn't a joke; this was for real. Nothing to be absorbed in slowly, but thrust upon her in a final, already decided way.

Part of her was crying out this can't be. We have the perfect life here. This is all a dream, a bad dream. I'll soon wake up. Rob had thrust a stack of papers into her hands, gave her a business card with the phone number of his attorney and was out the door. Her first instinct was to ask him to stay while they discussed the whole thing but he was gone.

Being stunned by the news slowly gave way to feeling the agony and the hurt of what had happened. She felt betrayed and angry and stupid because she hadn't seen it coming. And then she worried about whether or not she might have been exposed to AIDS or some other sexual disease. Should I have done more to please him? I should have tried harder. What did I do wrong? All of these feelings were to take turns in her mind especially over the next few days and weeks as she tried to sort out what had happened and what would happen to her for the rest of her life.

Later that first day, the conversation (or speech since she really wasn't given the chance to say anything) started to clear in her mind. He was gone. He would not be back. How could this be when they'd been together through high school, college, and twenty-six years of marriage?

Roz and Rob. Rob and Roz. The couple voted the cutest couple. Voted the king and queen of the prom. The couple voted the most likely to get married. The couple voted the most likely to stay married. Theirs was not a magical case of love at first sight. They had started together slowly, building a relationship on friendship, companionship, trust and loyalty, or so she had thought. They had similar goals, or so she had thought. She thought about Jeff and Jenny, their children. Is he turning his back on them, too? What will they think?

And what about his job? Why would he change employers? He'd been with the same pharmaceutical company since he had an internship with them while they were in college. He was a top salesman full of charm and charisma. He expected to be made a vice-president in the near future. She knew he'd become friendly with a member of the state legislature and this friendship had benefited the company greatly. This had also brought him to the attention of the lobbyists in Washington, D.C. Now he was on his way to join a firm there. Along the way he met a young intern at his firm and this had apparently resulted in an affair. After she graduated he bought a condo for them to share. How could she, Roz, have been so unaware of what was happening? He was home on weekends; he was home on holidays. Yet, he also had found time for another life, another woman, and now a baby on the way.

He wanted to do the right thing for the baby, he said, so he planned to go to the Caribbean, get a quickie divorce and move with his new bride to Washington, D.C. This would happen immediately. The right thing for his baby? Roz thought about that. What's the right thing for the woman he married and his children?

He'd arranged every detail. His lawyer, his good friend of many years, had already drawn up the papers *giving* her the house which he knew she would want to sell since it was so large and he might already have a buyer for it. Well, that answered one question - at least one other person knew about his affair - his lawyer. How many other people knew?

And what about their children? What would they think? They were young adults now already establishing their own lives. Jeff was good-looking, full of charm, and just married this past year to his college sweetheart. Jenny, their daughter, was getting ready to spend a year in Europe before making the final decision about a career. She'd learned several languages and was thinking about working for the U.N. Roz was proud of their children and happy for their successes. She didn't want to lean on them. They deserved better than having a lonely, crying mother dumped on their doorstep. How could she tell them? What words would she say? What close friend could she call? Her eyes filled with tears. After college she had worked for a large firm in Human Resources for more than a year. She quit that job to stay home with her family but after the children were in school she free-lanced as a Special Event Planner for several firms in the Chicago area. This occupation did not give her opportunities to form strong personal friendships or so she had told herself. She'd always considered herself a strong, independent woman who really didn't need those close tell-all relationships. But on that day she really wished she had that kind of friend. She didn't feel strong at all.

She had spent that day wandering from room to room, mostly crying and wondering what she could have done differently to keep this from happening. She loved her family, her home, her life. By evening she was sure it was all a bad dream; she would wake up in the morning and life would go on as usual.

That next morning, after Rob's speech, hearing the words from the voice on the radio, *the first day of the rest of your life,* reality set in. As she started to move through her day her first thought was to make a decision to do nothing at all until she had more time to think about it calmly and quietly. That was followed by a decision to see the attorney and get the whole thing over with as quickly as possible. That thought was followed by a decision that she would fight tooth and nail to hold her family together.

A phone call from her daughter who was checking to make sure her mom was OK after the big news of yesterday had stunned her.

"Did your father phone you?"

"Yea, he called and said he was leaving."

"Did you know about Barbi?"

"Yea. I saw them at the mall one day. They were having lunch together. Dad introduced me then."

"And you didn't think you should tell me?"

"He told me she was a colleague from work. I didn't suspect anything then but when I saw them a second time I began to figure things out."

"Why didn't you tell me?" Roz screamed out at her daughter for not telling her about Rob's affair. "You all must have thought I was pretty stupid."

"Oh, Mom, don't say that. I'm sorry. I didn't know what to do. I'm the one that felt stupid and embarrassed. I wondered if you knew about it and you were trying to work things out with Dad. Maybe you were trying to protect Jeff and me. Honest, Mom, I couldn't find the words to ask you about it. I didn't want to even think about what he was doing."

"I'll talk to you later, Jenny." She hung up, her head shaking with shame.

The next call came from Jeff. His voice was quiet as he spoke to his mother. "I guess Dad confessed everything, huh, Mom?"

"How long have you known about it?"

"Jenny saw them one day and told me. One day Dad invited Karen and me for lunch and she was there. Mom, she's younger than Karen. I felt embarrassed. I couldn't understand it then and I don't understand it now."

"Why didn't you tell me, Jeff?"

"At first I thought he was using her to feel young again. I thought maybe it was a one night thing and he'd get over it. Mom, can I ask you something? Do you think this was the only time he cheated on you?"

She felt stunned. "Do you know of any others?"

"No, and there was no point in asking him. I don't believe anything he says anymore. Karen and I want you to come and stay with us for a few days while you figure out what you'll do next. Will you come?"

For a moment, the desire to be cared for almost made her say yes. Feeling shame and embarrassment and a desire to hide, she declined his offer and said she'd talk with him later.

Roz was stunned to know her children had known for almost a year. She was angry for she thought she had a close relationship with her children. Jenny had said, "Mom, we didn't know Dad would leave you and why worry you about what might or might not happen?" Was it good or bad that this had happened? Roz had mixed feelings. Knowing that her children already knew about the affair was good because she hadn't had to say the awful words to them, which was a blessing, but it was hurtful that they knew something so painful and upsetting to her life yet said nothing.

She sat and read the papers he left behind. It appeared as he said it would be. The house would be hers, yet it was an expensive house to maintain: high taxes, high membership dues to their homeowner's association, high utility bills, etc. There was a high maintenance fee to take care of the grounds in the summer and the snow in the winter. Forget the country club fees. She'd never go there again. Did she really want to stay here? After thinking about it for a while, she decided she needed facts without any emotional baggage. She put in a call to their, or should she say his friend, Tom Wilson, the attorney.

"Hi, Mrs. Graham, we've been expecting your call," said the receptionist at Tom Wilson's law firm. "I'll put you right through."

"Roz. How are you?" She heard the cheery voice of Tom Wilson as if all was right with the world.

"Not very well, Tom. I think we need to talk. Can you see me tomorrow?"

"Of course. Why don't we meet for lunch at one o'clock?"

"I'd rather keep it business. Is one o'clock still OK?"

"Of course, of course. I'll see you then. Oh, by the way, Rob said you would be dropping off his suits at the cleaners. If you bring me the cleaner's ticket, I'll pick them up for you and see that Rob gets them."

Rob's suits? She had a faint memory of him telling her to drop them off as he had walked out the door. I guess I really was upset, she thought. I didn't remember it. Then she began to get angry. Why should I take them to the cleaners? If he wants them let him come and get them.

The next morning Roz wondered what clothes one is expected to wear when one is going to a meeting that will end her life as she knows it. She finally decided to be traditional and wear a black suit. Her eyes were still puffy and swollen so she spent some time trying to disguise the weariness and at least look somewhat presentable. She tried to plan what she would say - about fighting the divorce - about getting her own attorney....... She felt so overwhelmed that she had to sit down.

On her way the next morning she realized that she needed gas in her car. She pulled in at the station and pumped her gas but when she went to pay, the pump rejected her debit card. She pulled out her charge card. She was rejected again. What in the world can be wrong, she wondered as she paid for the gasoline with cash. Now I need to stop at the bank and get some money she thought. She entered the bank where she had been a regular customer for over twenty-five years.

"Mrs. Graham, the records indicate that this account is closed."

A sick feeling threatened to overtake her again. "There must be some mistake. I've had this account for years. I didn't close it."

The clerk smiled pityingly. "Let me get Mr. Martin, our manager, for you."

"Hi Roz, how are you this morning?"

Roger Martin's smile of pity was even more pronounced than the clerk's.

Oh, no, Rose thought. Does everyone in town know that Rob has left me? She tried to stay calm. "Roger, I seem to be having a problem." She tried to keep her voice strong and steady. "Both my debit and credit cards were declined this morning and now I'm told the account has been closed. What's going on? Are you having some computer problems?"

"I'm sorry Roz, I thought you knew. Rob closed all the accounts earlier this week."

"How can that be? Why wasn't I notified?"

"Roz, the accounts were all in Rob's name."

"But Roger, you opened the account for both of us. We sat right in your office and filled out the cards. I remember signing them."

He shifted uncomfortably. "Of course you were both here but everything was set up in Rob's name alone. Rob changed his mind after you signed the cards and put the accounts in his name. He said you were setting up your own account. I certainly thought you knew."

How naïve she had been. When she didn't speak, Roger reached out a consoling hand.

"Let me set you up a new account, Roz, so you'll have access to some funds today. We'll get this all straightened out."

No, she thought. *I'll* get this straightened out.

"Not today, Roger," Roz said as she left the bank.

Thank goodness, she thought, that I did set up my own account for my business. At least I have access to get cash to live on. Rob had always taken care of all the monthly bills and he had always kept some cash at the house that they both would use when they needed it. She had no idea she was not on the bank accounts. I guess this was his way to keep me under his thumb she thought. I wonder what other surprises are in store for me.

Tom was somewhat more subdued as she entered the attorney's office. His secretary brought in coffee.

"Tell me, Roz, did Rob really blindside you with this news. Did you suspect that something was happening?" Tom asked.

"Rob was very secretive. How long have you know about it?"

"Well, Rob seemed to be very smitten with Barbi from the first time he met her. I'm not sure when the affair started."

"Tell me, Tom, does your wife know about it? Do all of our mutual friends know?"

Tom looked a bit embarrassed as he admitted that they all knew. Rob had even brought Barbi to one of the events at the club when Roz had been out of town.

"But, Roz, I know that in his own way Rob loved you a lot. And in this settlement he's tried to be very generous with you. The house has increased tremendously in value; you can be set financially for life. The realtor appraised it for far over the expected amount and we may even have a buyer interested if you decide to sell."

"You already had the house appraised? You may already have a buyer for it? Sounds like you and Rob have thought of everything to get me out of the picture quickly," Roz snapped back.

"We were trying to make the transition easy for you," he replied nervously.

"Are you aware that my name is not on any of the bank and credit card accounts? Was it even legal for him to take my name off the accounts without my permission?"

Tom looked very uncomfortable. He shifted in his chair. "Rob did not intend for you to be in a bind. He set up new accounts that will be activated as soon as the divorce papers are signed."

She stood to leave.

"I'll have my attorney call you," Roz said feeling a bit of spirit find its way back into her life.

"If you want to sign the papers now there will be no need for you to go to the expense of an attorney," Tom told her.

She looked him in the eye and even felt a small smile come to her face. "That would be really foolish of me Tom," she said quietly and headed for the door.

"My wife wants to call you about lunch. She'll be in touch."

Roz paused, looking steadily at the old friend who now eyed her with such uncertainty.

"Tell her not to bother." Roz straightened her back and walked a bit taller out of the office.

The bravado left her as soon as she was out the door and with shaking legs she made her way to her car and burst into tears. She couldn't even think of the words to describe how she was feeling about the events of the day. That the man she had loved and trusted for so long had done these things to her was beyond her comprehension.

Many times before she had returned to an empty house but this time it was different. It seemed she heard her footsteps magnify as she walked in the door. She heard the hum of the refrigerator as it started to recycle. She heard the scratch of some branches that would need to be trimmed hitting the window and linking them all she heard the sounds of emptiness. No one who cared would ever be there so that she could call out to let them know she was home. She checked the answering machine. There was a call from Pat Wilson, Tom's wife. There were calls from two other of her friends, or maybe she should call them former friends. There was a call from her mother. Well, she could imagine that either Jenny or Jeff had called her mother with the news.

She decided not to answer any of those calls until evening, but when an hour later her mother again called, she picked up the phone. She might as well start to try to get used to discussing the upcoming divorce.

"Rosie, are you OK?" were the first words from her mother.

"Not really, Mom, but what choice do I have? Who called you; was it Jenny or Jeff?"

"Actually, it was Rob. I couldn't believe what he was telling me. You know how he wants to be in control of everything. I told him I was shocked at his behavior and would not talk to him. Now tell me, is this all really true?"

"I guess Rob is going his own way and right now and I don't know which way I'm going."

"I know which way you should go. Go to the airport and take the first plane to London. John and I would love to see you. Getting away from the area will give you time to think things through."

Rosalind thought for a minute and then declined the offer. Her mother then offered to come to her but Roz declined that offer also.

"I just need time to think about what is best. And it'll be best for me to do it in my own home."

They chatted briefly about Jeff and Jenny. Roz told her mother how hurt she was about the fact that both kids had known. "I can't believe they would let me live in this situation without knowing something this important."

"Well, Rob could always work his charm. The kids were used to his devious ways but they're good kids and wanted to believe their dad would come to his senses. Who knows how many lies he told them?"

"Mom, I've been such a fool."

"Roz, you are a bright, beautiful woman. You deserve better than that scumbag."

A bit more crying and commiserating and Roz hung up the phone.

Well, apparently, word was out - Roz has been dumped by Rob. She knew the phone lines must have been busy all week among their friends. Well, maybe in time she could think of them as friends. Not at this moment. She had never felt so alone.

The first days after her shock of the impending divorce had passed in a daze. She didn't sleep at night and was groggy all day. She didn't want to get dressed or eat. She refused to answer her phone unless it was Jeff or Jenny and those conversations were very curt and brief. One morning she was awakened from her daze by the incessant ringing of the doorbell. Go away, she thought, but there was no let-up. She finally made her way to the door, opened it and found Ann, her mother, and John waiting to be let in. Her mother wrapped her arms around her daughter and held her tight and all the tears started to flow. It felt so good to have someone hold her.

Finally with good humor John said, "I'm getting tired of holding the luggage. Would you two please move out of my way? I want to get to the kitchen and fix a cup of coffee."

As Roz was later to remember, the first stage of healing began at that moment. John seemed to know when to leave Roz and Ann alone and when to be there to listen; when to bring a cup of coffee or tea. John had always been a part of Roz's life. Her mother and father had been good friends with John and his wife and the families were very close. When Roz's father had died of a sudden heart attack when Roz was ten, it had been John and his wife who helped bring stability to her home. Shortly after, John's wife had been diagnosed with cervical cancer, and Roz's mother, Ann, had helped to take care of her good friend. It had been very natural when her mother and John had married the year after the death of his wife.

Roz, her mother, and John spent the first days rehashing what had happened, but finally John called a halt to the agonizing.

"I agree that Rob's a louse," John said finally after another day of tears. "It's time to think about you. What do you want to do? Do you want to stay in this big house with all the memories or make changes?" John asked. "You can have a whole new life."

"Tell me," he went on. "Have you seen an attorney yet?"

"Only Tom Wilson who is really Rob's attorney," she replied.

"Well, I'd recommend you see a different attorney to find out what options you might have. Think about what you really want. You might want Rob and your old life back but is that realistic? Think about what's important to you to have a new life. Maybe it's living in a certain way or certain friends. Maybe your job or maybe important people in your life that you want to stay near. Then ask yourself where you need to live to have that life."

Roz's mom said, "John, I think that's a good idea. Tom Wilson has been calling almost every day about the potential buyer he has for the house. At least thinking about what is important will help you decide whether or not you want to stay here. Do you know if any definite offers were made to buy the house?"

"No," Roz said. "I have all the papers he gave me but I haven't really looked at them. I don't think I can yet. But maybe you are right, John. Would you look at the papers first and then help me to understand them?"

"Of course," John said, "but are you sure you want me looking at all your personal papers. I think you should see an attorney."

"I guess I'll have to, but I'd like to have a better under-standing of them before I do. Maybe I'm not thinking clearly yet. I know I trust you and mom to help me think things through. I guess I'll have to accept that what I want, to go on with my life the way I thought it was, isn't going to happen. Maybe if I had seen things coming I could have tried to change things. But it's too late now."

"And maybe," her mother said, "you'll find that things were not always as good as you convinced yourself they were. You have good health and you are strong. You can come out of this and have a much happier life."

Roz made her mental list. Most of my friends are profes-sional friends. I really don't have personal friends I want to stay close with, she thought. And the house – well, it was a house chosen by Rob, furnished by Rob with the help of a profes-sional decorator. She hadn't been given very many opportuni-ties to give any input about it. She wasn't really tied to the area by her job. It was possible she could still work as a special events planner somewhere else. Or maybe she should return to the corporate world. Jeff was already married and Jenny would probably never live at home again. But where would she go? She remembered about a divorce attorney she had met when she planned a special event for one of the very large law firms. She had talked with the woman, Beverly Freeman, about what a sad job it must be to handle divorces. Beverly had said that it was sad, but sometimes rewarding because she would see an ex-spouse grow and become stronger. Roz decided to make an appointment with Beverly.

After reviewing the divorce papers drawn up by Rob's attorney, Beverly agreed with John's opinion. Even if Rob was a cad and louse, the settlement offered seemed to be fair. The house had appreciated considerably; the location was the best in the area. Rob had special annuities set up in her name. Financially, she should be set for life. But there are other sides to a divorce and if Roz wished to go ahead, Beverly would try to negotiate. But Beverly cautioned her, "I can't give you back your old way of life. Are the secrecy and the demands Rob makes the way you want to live your life? Without trust? I offer this word of advice. Statistics show that men who have this much power over women seldom change their behavior. Don't you think you deserve better?"

Roz left the office feeling numb. Of course I want to go back to my old life, she thought. It was so wonderful. Or was it? How often did Rob insist on going to the club when she was tired and wanted to stay in? How many times at the club did he leave her alone while he visited this group and then that one? How often had he turned down her request to come to some of the special events she planned? He had no interest in her career. He'd be angry with her when her events occurred on the same day as some of his plans. He used me and only wanted me around when it suited him. I'd become a trophy wife. Ready to be brought out and displayed when needed. And now a brighter, shinier, younger trophy wife had replaced her. Was I really happy or was I just content not to have to make a major change in my life? It was scary to think about life without him. But it was not very pleasant to think about life with him. He was quick to criticize her if she wore a favorite outfit too often. He told her she wore old lady clothes. Roz called her clothes professional. Her hair was never long enough or short enough.

Her thoughts were interrupted by the ringing of her cell phone. It was Rob.

"Why are you taking so long to sign the papers?"

"My attorney is reviewing them."

"You didn't need an attorney. There you go again, just wasting my money."

"Your money? You always said the money I earned was our money. I think…"

"Stop it, Roz. I need to get things settled. I told you to take my suits to the cleaners. Did you do it?"

For a brief moment a wave of panic swept over her body – *He'll be so mad. I should have remembered.* Then reality set in. "No, I didn't."

"Why not?"

"Why should I? You can take care of your own clothes." Then feeling a twinge of satisfaction she added, "Let Barbi be your slave."

"Little Roz is mad," Rob began in a singsong voice. His voice grew mean. "You'd better do it….."

"Goodbye, Rob."

"Roz," her mother greeted her when she returned home. "Tom Wilson is here."

"Roz. Good to see you again," Tom said smoothly. "I've been having a nice visit with your family."

"Well, Tom," Roz replied, almost rudely. "Let's cut to the chase. What brings you here?"

"Well, it's been a few weeks now and I haven't heard from you. I mentioned to you that there was a couple interested in buying your house if you decide to sell it. They're here in town on business and would like to see the house. I hate to rush you, but they're financially able to pay whatever you ask for it, and it seems a shame to possibly pass up this opportunity for them to see it."

"I haven't made any final decisions about what I'll do, Tom. And even if I do decide to sell the house I won't be rushed into doing it today."

"Well, could you at least let them see the house? They'll not be coming back to the states for three or four months."

"Let me have a couple of hours, Tom. I'll call you this afternoon."

After Tom left, Roz sat down with her mother and John. She told them about her visit to her attorney and her thoughts when leaving the office. John and Ann listened quietly and offered no opinions.

"Maybe it'd be OK just to let the couple see the house. Maybe they won't even like it and all this worry would be for nothing," Roz finally said.

John," she asked, "would you please call Tom and set up a time for the people to see the house?"

"Certainly," John answered. "Why don't we take a drive somewhere and have lunch on the day they come?"

"Wonderful idea," said Ann. "Why don't we drive up to the hill country and have lunch at one of those resort towns we used to visit? John, didn't your college roommate move up there year round?"

"Oh, yes, Don and Beth Cunningham liked the area so well they moved there permanently. How about it, Roz? Would it be OK to call them?" John asked.

Roz really didn't want to go but she could see how much her parents would enjoy the visit. And certainly there hadn't been much for them to enjoy since they'd been here.

"Yes," she said. "I've got to start living a life again some-day. Why not today?"

Chapter 2

The day was beautiful with spring waking up. Roz, John, and Ann left in the morning for the drive north. About three hours later they arrived at Nuna Lake. It was a charming little town in the hill country. At one time it was a resort area but over time it had become more of a year-round town. Don and his wife had purchased a summer home there many years ago. When he had a chance for an early retirement, they made it their permanent home.

The old friends were happy to reunite. Don had been an investment banker before his retirement and loved his work. He'd been retained as a financial advisor by a few old friends that he said kept him current with financial news and out of Beth's way.

The women sat on the big front porch that overlooked the lake and after the usual chitchat they talked about the decisions Roz would need to make.

"Why not move up here? This is a wonderful town. Small enough to be friendly and have people care. We've found most of the people here very respectful of your privacy but are here if you need them," Beth said. "I'm sure there are at least five or six houses on the market. Even if you only decided to stay a year, investment wise I think it would be good."

Roz replied, "Right now I'm not even sure I know how much money I could or should put into housing. I don't know if I could or should return to work. I guess I have a lot of don't knows."

"All of that takes time. You'll get the answers."

After a very pleasant day, on the ride home, John told Roz that he thought Don would be a good source for her to use for financial advice. Roz decided to take this advice and called Don upon arriving home.

Roz also made another decision – she'd like to move to Nuna Lake if she could find a house. She loved the serenity of just looking at the lake, at looking at the hills beyond it, of seeing nature around her. If she got a good price for her current house, she could take her time about deciding what to do with the rest of her life. She might miss the big city ways. Who knows, she might even miss some of her old business contacts. Right now she could not imagine ever missing her old friends. If I get too lonesome I can always move back to the city.

Tom Wilson called Roz the next day saying that the couple had loved the house, hoped to buy it as nearly furnished as possible, and made an offer to purchase.

"I need to know what you want me to do," Tom said. "If you're interested in selling I'd like to turn it over to a realtor. If you're absolutely not interested in selling, I'll advise them to look elsewhere."

"I guess this is decision time," Roz said after hanging up the phone. "I do think I want to sell and move to Nuna Lake. I wish I could get the opinions of Jeff and Jenny. I haven't really talked with them since Rob left."

"I think you should talk with them," her mother said. "Why not call the kids and ask them here for dinner? Don't you think it is time to face them? Anyhow, John and I will be returning to London soon and I'd really like to see them."

Another step forward, Roz thought. As much as she hated to admit it, it might be easier to have that first meeting with the children while her mother and John were there.

"Yes, you're right," Roz said. "I'll call them now."

The first meeting with her grown children started off fairly stiff and formal, but within a few minutes, everything seemed normal. She realized how much she loved and missed her children. They both had a gift of gab and made friends easily. Jeff was tall, looked like his father and had his father's ways to say the politically correct thing. But there was a quiet, gentle side to him, unlike his dad. He was self-assured, not seeming to need a lot of people or things. Jenny looked like her mother but like her father, she was a stranger to none; bubbly, enthusiastic, eager to live life to the fullest. Because she had a real talent for learning foreign languages she said she wanted to make the world a better place.

"I missed you, Mom," Jenny said. "I thought that maybe you were really mad at me for not telling you about Dad. He's such a jerk. I never thought Dad would want a divorce."

Roz embraced her daughter, held her tight.

Jeff held her tighter and longer than usual and told her how much he loved her. Karen, his wife, clung to Roz. With tears in her eyes she told Roz that she admired her for staying so calm through it all. Roz hoped that Karen's words were sincere since she didn't think she had acted calmly. Staying at home crying, not answering the phone, not really able to make decisions, was she turning away from those whom might have wanted to be her friend?

After dessert Roz told the children that the house was now hers. She told them she had an offer from a prospective buyer. Did they think she should sell, and if so, where should she go? Jeff and Karen immediately said she should sell and buy a condo close to them. Jenny seemed a bit more wistful about the house, but said that if her mom always made sure to have an extra bedroom for her to come home to she would support whatever her mother wanted to do.

When the house was quiet that evening, as she, her mother and John sat talking, a feeling of peace came over Roz. Knowing her children were supportive, feeling the love from her mother and John, Roz knew the days ahead would be hard but she would somehow get through them. She felt the tears welling in her eyes. For nearly thirty years Rob had been a part of her life. I can't pretend it didn't happen, she thought. She remembered their wedding day. But she also remembered how Rob had told her to stand just a little straighter when they were in the reception line. He often did that to both Roz and Jenny. As she thought about that day, she realized that was the day he'd started to control her. Or was it? She probably let him control her while they were dating. I wanted so badly to please him, she realized. I do deserve better. She admitted to herself what she had been afraid to say.......my marriage is over. It's time now to make it official.

As Roz prepared for bed that evening, she made a mental note to call Beverly Freeman in the morning. She would sign the papers to end her marriage.

She made two other calls the following day, one to Tom Wilson, advising him that she would sell, and the second to Don Cunningham, asking him if he would refer her to the local realtor in Nuna Lake.

Things had moved very quickly after that. Don told her of a couple of homes on the market at Nuna Lake that he felt would be worth her time to look at and made arrangements for her to see them.

Both houses had been built as summer homes. One was a small cottage. There was a small wall around a large courtyard filled with old-fashioned flowers. The grassy yard was small with beautiful blossoming trees landscaping the area. The house itself had been updated and well maintained. There was a big family eat-in kitchen, a family room with a huge fireplace filling one wall. There were two good-sized bedrooms with windows on two walls. A basement and attic provided storage areas. This house might be just the right size, Roz thought. Jeff's married and Jenny will probably never live at home again.

The other house looked like it was set in a jungle. The trees and shrubs were all overgrown. The driveway was nearly hidden. The house, set on about a ten acre plot, had four bedrooms upstairs and a huge open first floor. It had been a beautiful summer home at one time; had a wonderful view of the lake and a wrap-around porch on three sides. There was a screened porch upstairs large enough to sleep on if the night was hot, and a large turret room in the attic with a beautiful view of all sides of the property. There was gingerbread trim on the house. At one time the house had been painted white, but now it was a weathered gray. As Roz walked through the rooms she could imagine having gauzy curtains on the window that you could see through and let them cool you as they moved in the breeze. Although some rewiring and plumbing had been done, Roz knew there would be a lot more work to do. Roz stood on the porch and looked at the lake. There were two sailboats on the horizon and smaller boats closer to shore. Roz fell in love with the view and the house. It made her choice became easy in spite of the jungle. Don thought it was a wise choice as an investment. With some needed repairs he felt it would appreciate in value. Roz saw a lot of possibilities for restoring it to its old beauty. An added bonus was the fact that the house was about to go into foreclosure and the price had been greatly reduced. Don assured her that her budget would cover the cost of updating the house.

No one had lived in the house for fifteen years or more. It had been sold four years earlier. The new owners had never moved into the house. They had the plumbing and electrical brought up to code, and began to update the kitchen and baths. Then they found out they would be leaving the country for about five years so decided to sell the property. There was still a lot of work to be done. Roz decided the first steps had to be to clear the property, especially the trees, for some looked as if a strong wind would blow them over and even now you could barely get in the driveway. Don recommended she contact Mike Nelson, the local guru of trees.

Mike Nelson was one of those ageless men. He was a tall, strong man who would probably look the same age for thirty years. His hair had just a hint of gray at the temples and his skin was already starting to tan for the summer. He had been born at Nuna Lake and knew the history of every house. He loved nature, graduated from Stanford University with degrees in Landscape Architecture and Botany and had returned to town to establish a nursery and landscape business. He agreed to meet with Roz to formulate a plan to make the property livable.

"This house was the most beautiful in Nuna Lake for years," he told Roz. "The family who owned it had colorful gardens for every season. It'll be a real pleasure to restore the grounds. Do you plan to live here year round or just spend summers here?"

"Year round," Roz told him. "And I know nothing about taking care of yards."

"Well, that's why you hire me," he said with a smile. "I suggest we clear the brush so you can get to the house and garage and then trim the trees to make them safe. After you have lived here a month or so we'll make a plan to landscape it to suit your needs for the house. Are you planning to open a Bed and Breakfast?"

"Oh, no. I'll be here alone. Your plan sounds great since I do need to move in fairly quickly. I sold my home in the city and would like to get settled here."

"How soon do you plan to move in," he asked.

"Hopefully, I can move within the month."

"I think that's great. Nuna Lake is a great place for a new

start. We have our own character*s* here, and I guess I'm one of them, but it's a wonderful, caring community. I'd like to be the first to officially welcome you here."

With smiles and a warm handshake they completed their deal.

When she got home she phoned Jeff and Jenny telling them her news and suggested that if there were things in the home they would like to have, this was the time to tell her. She invited them to take a trip with her to Nuna Lake to see the house and told Jenny she could choose a bedroom in the new house and take any furniture she wanted.

When they arrived in Nuna Lake to see the house, Roz was pleased to see the driveway and much of the brush had been cleared. Work was underway to repair and refinish the floors. The finishing work on electrical and plumbing had been completed on the kitchen and bathrooms. Jeff and Jenny were very excited for Roz and began to advise her where to place the piano, the perfect place for the telescope, etc. The new floors were beautiful and Roz knew her area rugs would fit the area and complement the stained glass windows throughout the house. The young people saw possibilities that even Roz had not had time to think about. Their excitement for her and their plans to visit often brought joy to her. They found the garage had been made into a storage area and they created stories about all the treasures and wealth that was sure to be hidden in there. When they stopped for lunch at the local cafe, Jenny, as usual, knew no strangers and by the time lunch was over, most of the patrons had stopped by to meet their new neighbor.

Roz knew that Jenny would be leaving with her college roommate, Carrie, for a year in Europe before the middle of July and thought of waiting until after that time to move, but instead decided to move up to Nuna Lake at the end of June. She was very surprised when Jenny phoned with a request.

"Mom, I have a big favor to ask of you. I was telling Carrie about your new house. We're planning a last camping trip with

Nick and Marty on the Fourth of July. We'd like to come to Nuna Lake instead. Would that be OK?"

"Jenny, you know I won't have the bedrooms settled that quickly, but if you don't mind roughing it a bit I'd love to have all of you come up."

"We'll have our sleeping bags. We'll camp out in the yard. I want them to see the lake. Anyhow, I brought home a brochure and there's a lot going on in town on the holiday. We thought it would be fun to check it out."

Roz decided her top priority was to purchase a lot of food and forget about unpacking.

The group arrived around lunchtime and explored the property and the woods beyond it. Then Jenny asked for the key to the garage to explore all the treasures that she expected to find there. The first thing they dragged out was an old porch swing. They decided to hang it on the front porch. The chains were rusty, the wood was splintered, but with great fun and advice from each other, they hung the swing.

"See, Mom, what a great contribution we're making to your home," Jenny said.

Roz quietly hoped the chains would hold and no one would be injured.

That night the group slept in the yard in their sleeping bags. Roz heard them talking and laughing far into the night. She was glad the divorce had not had a greater impact on her daughter and that Jenny still found pleasure in her life. She knew that this would be the last time the four young people would be together for a year, or maybe even forever. They'd all been close friends through three years of college but now Jenny and Carrie would be completing their last year abroad. It was an exciting time for all of them.

Nuna Lake really celebrated the Fourth of July. A Street Fair was being held in town and the celebration started with a parade made up mostly of local organizations and fire trucks. The afternoon featured *Fun at the Lake* with swimming, water skiing, paddleboats and jet skiing available. There was a fishing contest, a beauty contest for Miss Nuna Lake and a beautiful baby contest. A big community dinner was held in the park at six o'clock followed by an outdoor concert and then fireworks after dark.

The young people were up early and in a great mood. They said they'd never seen so many stars as they had seen during the night. The breeze from the lake made for excellent sleeping. They tried to get Roz to join them for the festivities but she sent them on their way. She promised them she would consider joining them for the fireworks.

Just after they left, she heard a car pull into the driveway. She saw Mike Nelson as she made her way to the door.

"Hi," he said. "I saw your family leaving without you and decided to drop off these plans for your landscaping. You don't have to look at them today, but after you get a chance to review them we can meet again. I hope you don't mind that I'm interrupting your holiday."

Roz laughed as she told him that only one member of the group was her family. She could see that he was eager for her to see the plans so invited him in for coffee. As they sat at the kitchen table with their coffee and the plans, she realized how much thought and care for the environment he put into his work. He told her he'd visited the house often as a child and how it appeared to be a house full of joy. Many community events were held on the lawn. His enthusiasm was contagious and Roz saw the possibilities for making it a beautiful home. But when he asked her if she wanted to take care of the flower plantings, she had to admit she knew nothing about gardening. He told her he would teach her but everyone needed to do some of their own planting to make it their garden.

The day passed quickly for Roz. From time to time she looked out on the lake and imagined that she picked out her family among the crowd at the beach. About nine-thirty that evening, they returned home to pick up Roz to take her to the beach to watch the fireworks. They had a wonderful day on the water. Their bodies were browned from the sun. But after the day's activities and then attending the concert, they were tired. When Roz told them she'd decided not to go, they decided they would stay home and watch the fireworks from the porch. The view was beautiful with the reflections of the fireworks on the lake. It was a fitting finale to a wonderful day for them. When Roz went to bed she could hear them laughing and talking about the day. As she thought about it, she remembered about other times when her children had crowds at the house. This was different. They were all adults now. Their joy came from having a fun filled day, of being together maybe for the last time. In the morning they would head back to the city. The girls would be leaving for New York to join the group they would be traveling with and the boys had summer jobs. Roz said a prayer of thanks that she had this opportunity to see her daughter and her friends. She knew that after a year away Jenny would be changed. She felt sad for a moment that Rob was missing this phase of Jenny's life. But that was the choice he made.

After they were gone the next morning she again looked at the plans Mike had made. They really were special and Roz began to be excited about how beautiful it would all be.

"Is your name Roz or is that a nickname for Rose," Mike had asked her.

"It's really Rosalind but my dad always called me Rosie."

"I'm happy to hear that because I think we should restore the old rose garden for Rose."

"What a nice idea," she said.

She didn't see any changes she would want to make to the plans. If Mike is as good as he appears to be her yard should be spectacular.

She decided she liked the porch swing the young people had uncovered in the garage but was still worried about its safety so she stopped at the hardware store while she was out getting a few groceries.

"Mrs. Graham, I'm Harry Moore and I own this store. Welcome to Nuna Lake. Anything we can do to help you get settled?" he asked.

"Well, as a matter of fact there is." Roz told him about finding the old swing. She expected he might tell her about someone who could fix it for her or even sell her a new one. But instead he told her he would be happy to tell her what she needed so she could restore it - sandpaper, paint and paint brushes and new chains. As Roz left the store with her supplies she wondered if she, Roz Graham, who had never done anything like this in her lifetime, could really do it.

At the same time she was excited about trying something new. She wondered if everyone in town did things for themselves. She'd been used to having everything done for her. Now Mike had her planting flowers and Harry had her restoring a swing. Well, she knew her life was changing. How big a mess could she make of things?

Over the next few weeks, she managed to get things settled and stored away in the house. She decided to paint the bedroom walls. Once again she turned to Harry. After helping her select the paint and supplies she needed, he offered to come to her house the next morning to help her get started in one room.

"You won't need me after the first five minutes," he told her, "but I'll be there to give you the confidence you need to get started."

He was right. That evening she felt very successful looking into the bedroom she had just finished painting a pale green. It looked beautiful and she did it. She would try another room the next day.

The landscaping was going well. Almost every day Mike sent a couple of strong young men to work on one part or another. Her swing project had gone well. She bought some white wicker furniture with brightly colored cushions for the front porch. Each morning she would take her morning cup of coffee and the morning newspaper and sit out there. The sunset on the lake in the evening was magnificent.

She didn't wander very far from her home. She still had many moments of hurt, anger, and disappointment. The people in town were very friendly but Roz wasn't yet ready to let them into her life. Her world mainly consisted of the landscaping crew and a few other people she had in for various chores. There was Mike and Harry who were so helpful. Every time Roz wanted to try something new to restore, she turned to Harry. Many of the women in town introduced themselves to her when she shopped but Roz always told them she was too busy to stop for a cup of coffee today, maybe next time. She had decided not to risk getting too close to anyone and maybe being hurt.

Late that fall, Mike showed up with a basket of bulbs and a few tools. He had to be out of town for a week or so but said it was time that she planted the bulbs. She told him she had no idea how to plant them. He showed her the place off the back patio where they were to go and showed her how to plant them. "Next spring you'll be very pleased and happy you did this," he told her.

When Thanksgiving approached, Roz made up her mind she would cook a small turkey and all the traditional goodies even if she were alone. Having done that (and it wasn't as bad as she thought) she began to think of Christmas. Did she really want to spend it alone? She knew she could go to London to be with her mother and John. Jenny and Carrie would be there. Jeff and Karen invited her to join them in New York with Karen's family. She decided to stay home. She shopped and mailed packages and put up a small tree. Usually, this was a busy time for her at work, planning so many big corporate Christmas parties. She missed the excitement and the people contact. Coming to Nuna Lake was the right move but she felt she wanted a little more during this season. She decided she would go to church on Christmas Eve. She got her coat and attended the midnight service. She enjoyed the music and hearing the Christmas story once more. She enjoyed all the friendly greetings there in spite of the fact that she had tried to sneak in and go to the balcony.

She spent the winter doing some decorating in her house, unpacking boxes, reading many of her favorite classics, e-mailing to her family, especially Jenny, taking long walks. One day she spent the entire afternoon at the piano. She played all her old favorites.

One morning she awoke with a bad headache, runny eyes and nose, and a stuffed head. Oh, no, she thought. Not a nasty cold. It had been years since she had one and this seemed to be a bad one. She tried some hot lemon tea and some leftover chicken soup but nothing she tried made her feel better. She went back to bed but was uncomfortable there. She was really having a bad day. After pacing the floor for most of the day she thought she'd like to put on an old, shabby flannel bathrobe that she had saved for days like this. Now, if she could just remember where she stored it. She found it finally in one of the spare closets on the top shelf. Beside it on that shelf was a large brown envelope.

She remembered that she had been unpacking some boxes when the man doing her flooring had handed her the envelope, telling her he had found some papers under the floorboards in the upstairs bedroom and saved them for her. Roz had forgotten all about it.

She reached inside and drew out a book that appeared to be a journal or diary. The book was covered with sawdust and some cobwebs. Roz carefully turned the pages which were brittle with age. She found no name or date on it. She laid it on the table by the chair in her bedroom and lit a fire in the fireplace. She put on her old robe and her oldest warm slippers. She made a pot of chamomile tea and fixed some crackers and jam on a tray and returned to her bedroom. The fire looked warm and comforting as sleet and ice hit the windows outside. As she had her tea and crackers she opened the book.

The first few pages contained some poetry; lovely poems about the peaceful environment around her. As Roz read on she decided that it definitely was written by a woman, a lonely woman. From references made to various things, Roz decided this woman was used to living a life surrounded by friends and family. It was almost as if the book were written in code. No names were ever used, just initials. There was a feeling of loneliness in the writings even though the writer seemed to be surrounded by people.

G. and her children are here this week. She brought a letter from J. He will not be coming up this weekend. That will make three weekends this month he has not come up. But I would rather be up here than in the hot city. It is so beautiful here. And peaceful. N. is thriving here, getting spoiled by everyone but is still a kind child and learning so many things about nature and animals that she could not learn in the city. G. is staying in the guest house. She also brought along her tennis instructor. He'll stay in his own cottage but I wonder......... R. is also here staying in a guest bedroom. Now we will have four for bridge each evening after dinner. My favorite time of each day is when I'm outside walking through our grounds or in the woods. The beauty almost changes day to day. M. is teaching me so much about flowers. I know he keeps watch over everything here which makes me feel safe.

....

We had a big storm last night with a lot of wind. I got really frightened. But when I looked out the window I saw M. walking around in the storm. I called out to him and told him to come in out of the weather but he said he just wanted to be sure everything was OK.

....

31

Another week, different guests. I'm glad they find their own entertainment each day. And it does help N. to learn social skills. I have started a new routine. Each day I fix some coffee and pastries and M. and I share them together under a tree or in the woods. He is a very intelligent man which surprised me since he claims he has never left this area. But he certainly knows about people. I saw B. flirting with him the other day. He had to be aware of it but he just quietly kept her at arms length.

....

M. kissed me today. It just happened. We both know it shouldn't have happened. I must be very careful. I am married to J. He is a good man.

....

J. came up for a week. I am feeling so guilty. He is so good to me and he really loves N. I should have been able to have a dozen children. J. has so much respect for M. He tried to get M. to come for dinner but, as always, M. chooses not to come into our home. What am I going to do?

....

M. and I said goodbye today. I will be leaving to go back to Chicago in the morning. I will never forget M. or how I felt lying in his arms. I must stop remembering this or I can never go back to Chicago. And I must go back for the sake of my daughter. J. would never let her live up here year round. M. could never, never be happy in the city. I must make this sacrifice and be satisfied to live with my memories. Until next summer...........

Roz was weeping as she read the entries. Such private thoughts. Who could imagine this book would be found all these years later? She wondered if the affair ended there. As she dried her eyes she started to laugh. I guess I have been having a pity party, she thought. But I do feel better now. Roz carefully wrapped the book in tissue papers, put it in a box and put the box away in the closet. Someday I'll make a decision about what to do with it, she thought. Maybe it would be best to destroy it and keep the secrecy and privacy of the writer. But it was interesting to read about the guest cottages and playing tennis. The original owners must have owned nearly all the property in Nuna Lake.

One sunny morning as spring approached, she walked out on the patio and found the first little shoots of the spring bulbs breaking through the ground. Just like those new bulbs, I'm going to break my old habits and start my new life, she thought.

As she sat on her porch a year later after that dreadful day, she thought about the changes in her life as she sipped her coffee. I'm doing OK. Maybe someday I'll call my old friends. The ringing of her phone interrupted her thoughts. She hurried inside to take the call.

"Hi, Roz. This is Judy Martin. My mother is visiting me and I'd love to show her your beautiful spring garden. It's getting to be the talk of the town. We'd love to see it. Could I bring her by this afternoon?"

"Hello, Judy" Roz answered. "You're so nice to tell me that. I'd be pleased to have you come by, but I have a better idea. Would you both be free to come for lunch? We'll just have something light and since it's such a beautiful day, we can eat out on the patio among the flowers."

"Are you sure, Roz? This is such short notice."

"Really, it will be fun. Is noon OK?"

"That sounds great. We'll see you then."

As Roz hung up the phone she couldn't believe she'd actually invited someone to her home. It would be the first time in over a year she'd invited anyone for more than a cup of coffee. Maybe, just maybe, she was starting to move on.

Fortunately, she had mixed up a batch of refrigerator roll dough yesterday so she brought it out and pinched off enough dough for a dozen rolls, and set them to rise. She had plenty of chicken left over for a big chicken salad. With some fresh fruit and homemade cookies, she could fix an easy lunch.

She was surprised to find she was really enjoying getting out her pretty plates and cups. She cut a small bouquet of flowers for a centerpiece. She glanced out the patio doors and was pleased with the picture she saw. This area had turned out even better than she'd hoped. A low wall had been built around the edge of the flagstone patio and masses of spring bulbs had been planted atop it. Behind them were azalea and forsythia plants getting ready to bloom. All of this was against the background of a green lawn that went into the woods behind the house. The woods were also in bloom, with branches of buds which were a light green. The scene made her feel full of joy and hope.

Judy and her mother, Bess, arrived promptly at noon. Judy was about Roz's age, full of energy and enthusiasm. Roz had met her in the grocery store when Judy had approached her to introduce herself and welcome her to the neighborhood. Prior to today their only contact had been at the store. Roz's neighbors had seemed to understand and respect her need for privacy, and while she had received a few invitations no one put pressure on her to accept. Bess was an older version of Judy. With a big smile she thanked Roz for the chance to see the flowers and the invitation for lunch.

As Roz greeted her guests and started the short yard tour, the old graciousness, which had been a part of her life hosting so many dinner parties, came back to her like an old friend. She was really enjoying this.

"This wall has made such a nice addition and the flowers are beautiful. Some of the neighborhood kids have been sneaking looks from the hillside in the woods. Word has gotten all over town about the park you are creating," said Judy.

Roz admitted that she'd enjoyed the project. "But I did have help from Mike Nelson at the nursery. He is knowledgeable about how to trim the trees and bushes to help them be healthy. He pointed me in the right direction for purchasing bulbs and planting them to get the most benefit from the sun. But I did do all the digging and planting last fall. It's my first try at gardening."

"Mike Nelson's a gem," said Judy, "and he loves Nuna Lake. I think he's taught just about everybody in Nuna Lake how to plant flowers."

Roz brought the hot rolls and the rest of the lunch to the patio along with a huge pot of hot tea. She felt herself warming up to her new friends. Roz had a little concern that the conversation might turn personal. She didn't know if she was ready for that. She need not have worried. They discussed fashion in clothes all the way from Bess's days when one got dressed up to go to the store, to today's shorts and halters and crop tops. And the way blue jeans have become ageless. They discussed hair styles and music and Bess had them laughing as she told them about winning a jitterbug contest, and also having her very tight-fitting bodice on a full skirted dress rip apart at a square dance. It's been a really nice day, Roz thought after they left. It was nice to have people around. Maybe with the bitterness of the last year I had built a wall around myself to try to keep from being hurt even more she thought. Maybe, some of those phone calls those first days could have been calls from friends who really did want to be there for me. But I shut the door. Well, that's in the past she thought. We all need other people in our lives. Today, I really did take a step toward the rest of my life. I did make some good decisions. The move to this community was good. And I love this house.

When she sat out on her porch and watched the sunset that evening, she recalled the past year with all of the surprise, sadness, and confusion it had brought. But she found she felt stronger, more independent, and happier than she had been for many years when she lived in the shadow of Rob - always afraid that what she did might not please him.

Chapter 3

That night she slept better than she had for years and when she awoke to the familiar greeting of "Gooood Morning America, this is the first day of the rest of your life," she was ready to respond back, "You bet it is. And it will be a good one."

As she made her way to the porch with her cup of coffee, she decided to take a pad of paper and a pen with her. If this is a new year for me, she thought, I should make some New Year Resolutions. Getting out into the real world should be first, and people contact had to be there, too. She started her list:

Say thank you to the people who have helped me this year.

Join a group.

Contact an old acquaintance.

Well, maybe that last one would be a bit of a stretch but the first two should be easier. She began to think of all the people who had helped her. Mike and Harry were at the top of the list followed by the grocer who had called to see if she was OK when she hadn't come in that week, and the woman at the card shop who was always so cheerful and made time to serve a cup of coffee in the back room. And there was Joe who faithfully came to clear her driveway each time it snowed and the crew that cut her lawn. She thought of Lois, the librarian who always kept the current best sellers available for her. Well, at least that's a start, she thought, but how could she do it? Well, I'll think of something, she told herself.

Roz thought about joining a group. Should she take a class or join a book club? Lois had told her the club at the library was very interesting with a mix of people who attended. It made for good discussions. She really should be more regular about going to church and not try to sneak in the back door to go to the balcony. She always felt renewed when she went to church. She used to love to sing in the church choir. Or maybe she should take piano lessons again or at least practice every day. At one time she was fairly good. Maybe she could give piano lessons to beginners.

Was she ready to contact a former friend? Maybe it would be good to let them see how well she was doing. And let them know she was a survivor.

She decided to start with Harry. She had heard through idle chatter that his wife had been ill but she didn't know the cause. She decided to bake a lemon pie and take it to him to share with his wife. She headed immediately to the kitchen and got busy. That afternoon, she drove to the hardware store and found Harry just leaving for home. She handed him the pie as she thanked him for his help during the last year.

"Mrs. Graham, may I call you Rose?" he asked. "You're always so pleasant when you come here. You're so open to suggestion and always polite. This is very kind of you. It shows what a lady you are. It wasn't necessary for you to do this. But I want you to know that just last night my Millie told me a piece of lemon pie would taste so good. I think the good Lord was watching out for me for she hasn't been hungry for anything for weeks now."

"Harry, of course call me Rose I'm glad if my timing was good today. Did I hear right, that your wife has been ill?"

"Yes, she has had some heart problems and at our age, it is taking a bit longer to get over them. She isn't able to do much and really misses being in the kitchen to fix the extra things we like. I've been doing a lot of the cooking and I'm not such a good cook. This pie will really be special."

As Roz left the store she thought, well, that is one more person to call me Rose. "Hey, maybe I'm as beautiful as a rose," she laughed to herself. I think I have made a new friend, not just an acquaintance.

Maybe she made two friends. That evening she received a phone call from Millie, thanking her for the pie. "It tasted wonderful. I've had no appetite for so long I forgot how good something can taste. As soon as I get on my feet again, I do hope you'll come for dinner some evening. I really am looking forward to meeting you. Harry has told me you're such a kind person."

"You're much too nice," Roz responded. "I'm afraid I have been a bit of a recluse since I moved here and not very friendly."

"That is not so," Millie said. "You're just another person making a new path for your life. It takes time. I do hope we can become better acquainted."

"Me, too," answered Roz. "And I'll make sure that happens."

The next morning, after having her wake-up cup of coffee, Roz decided that she needed to make some plans. What? Make plans? I haven't done that for a long time, she thought. But in spite of the fact that she had settled in quite nicely there were things she hadn't done. Like unpacking a lot of boxes stored in the basement. And there was the garage/storage area. She still could not put her car in the garage as she had only taken out the porch swing and a small table that she had refinished with Harry's help. Who knows, I may find another treasure, she thought. And of course she needed to drive into town for some fresh vegetables and fruit. She also had a book due at the library and she needed a few birthday cards. "Maybe I'll do the errands first," she said to herself.

After a bite of breakfast and a quick shower she left the house. But before she could get to her car, her eyes were drawn to one of her many flower gardens. Blue and yellow columbines with their light lacy stems were moving gently in the breeze in front of the blue and yellow irises standing up straight and strong. In the front of the flower bed the blue and yellow pansies with their little faces were reaching for the sun. How beautiful, she thought as she got into her car. When these flowers were done blooming, other blue and yellow flowers would take their place. Flowers like blue bells, wishbones, and delphiniums and sunshine daisies. And she knew that as the season got warmer she'd have many more beautiful plantings to enjoy. Mike had encouraged her to plan her gardens so that she would have something blooming all season long.

First she stopped at the library where Lois greeted her and told her she had been saving the latest best seller for her. Next stop was Sarah's, the card shop.

The bell that announces customers rang as the entered the store but Roz saw no one there. Usually Sarah, a woman in her late twenties with shoulder-length warm brown hair pulled back into a ponytail, greeted everyone.

"Hello," Roz called out as she entered.

"Oh, Mrs. Graham," she heard. "Please help me. I'm in the back room."

Roz hurried back and found Sarah Myers lying on the floor in great pain. She hurried to her as she grabbed her cell phone from her purse. "What happened?"

"I fell from the ladder and I think I've broken my ankle," she answered. "I'm afraid to get up."

"Lie still," Roz advised her. "I'm calling for help. We'll get you to the hospital in no time."

"No, no, I can't go yet. I'm expecting a special shipment this morning and if I don't sign for it they'll return it. There's no one I can bring in today. Julia is out of town and Katy is in school." Julia was Sarah's only full time help.

Already Roz could hear sirens in the background as the paramedics made their way to the store. "Just tell me what to do and I'll stay here and sign for the shipment," she told Sarah.

"Oh, I couldn't ask you to do that."

"You're not. I'm volunteering. Now tell me what to do."

As soon as Sarah was on her way to the hospital Roz started to look around in the shop. There were cards for all occasions as well as gift items, all tastefully displayed with just the right touch of class. After the package had arrived and Roz had signed for it, she was not sure if she should close up shop or keep it open for a while. She had one customer who had the exact amount of cash for her purchase. About noon, the bell rang and in came Katy, the high school sales help.

"Hi, Mrs. Graham," she said cheerfully. "My mother heard about Sarah and came to school to tell me. Are you getting along OK here? Can I show you how to ring a sale? I have a few minutes before my afternoon classes start and I can come back as soon as classes are over around three. Will you be OK till then?"

"Well, I guess so," Roz responded as Katy proceeded to instruct her on ringing sales.

Just then the phone rang. It was Sarah calling from the hospital. She had broken her ankle but it was a small fracture and a clean break. Recovery should be swift. But she was worried about the shop. Katy assured her that she would come in after school to close and Julia would be back tomorrow. Roz agreed to stay for the afternoon until Katy came back.

Roz took on a new approach as customers arrived that afternoon. In addition to quite a few cards, she sold several gift items. This is fun she thought and a very nice way to meet people.

When Katy returned, Roz bought a pot of tulips and left

for the hospital to drive Sarah home. As Roz made her way back to her own home, she realized that she had volunteered to help out in the shop until Sarah would be back. Did I really volunteer to do that, she wondered? Well, who knows? I might enjoy it.

The next day when Roz stopped by the shop she found Julia busy unpacking a new shipment of gifts that had come in. Julia was a middle-aged flower child. She was of medium height and had a thick head of hair streaked with gray that reached just below her shoulders. She always wore the same style clothes; long full brightly colored skirts with a peasant blouse or an oversized shirt. She wore sandals on her feet all year round. Her granny glasses either hung on a chain around her neck or on the end of her nose. She loved people and her job at the shop. She examined each piece she removed from the shipping boxes for nicks or chips, and made a special place for storage of anything not placed on the shelves. Roz pitched in to help Julia. When customers stopped by, Roz was there to greet them. Word had gotten out about Sarah's accident and many people just wanted to know how she was. The time passed quickly as Roz found out when suddenly Katy came in after her afternoon classes. Roz decided she should take Julia out for a late lunch. As she drove home later that afternoon she realized she had met more people that day than she had in all the months since she had moved to Nuna Lake. And the people were so nice.

The next day as she and Julia tidied up the shop, the bell rang and a tall man wearing safari type slacks with lots of pockets, a long sleeved shirt and a safari type hat came into the store. Roz approached him to ask if he needed help.

"I certainly do," he said. "I'm shopping for a few gifts for some special people in the area. But I want each one different and I want each of them to be special."

The customer was a writer doing research in the area for a new book and he wanted to thank those people who had helped him. Roz asked him questions about each person. One gift was for an old Cherokee Indian whose ancestors had roamed the area many years before the white men had settled there. For him they chose a beautiful hand carved wooden bird that was native to the area. For Mrs. Kingsman, who knew every bird and critter in the area and was the local expert on bird watching, they chose a watercolor painting of a bird in its natural habitat. Roz chose a leather portfolio for old Mr. Markham who for years had maintained all the township business and cemetery records. There were a few other gifts, also, including a search for something special for the granddaughter of the Cherokee man. She loved her grandpa and was always by his side. For this little girl they chose a music box that was a figurine of an old man with his granddaughter at his knee.

By the time they had chosen the gifts Will and Roz were on a first name basis. "Now," he said, "let me take you to lunch to thank you for all the personal shopping you helped me with."

Roz started to protest, but Julia urged her on and said she would wrap each gift while they were gone. Roz finally left with Will for the local eatery. Will was charming and thoughtful. He was on a first name basis with the staff at the diner as he was in town quite often.

As they walked back to the card shop Will said, "This has been fun. You are a very interesting person. I'm glad to get to know you. We must get better acquainted." Rose told him that would be nice.

The next couple of weeks passed quickly but Roz kept her mind on her self-help list. Say a thank you, join a group, and contact an old acquaintance.

As she looked around her beautiful yard, she decided to call Mike Nelson and invite him and his wife to dinner that weekend.

"Hi Mike, it's Roz Graham. I love my yard so much I'd

like to say a proper thank you. Are you and your wife free to come for dinner Saturday night?"

"Hi Rose," he answered. "It's very nice for you to invite me and I'm available but there is no wife. But I have a teen-age son who loves to come to your house. Might I bring him instead?"

"Of course," she said. "Your son has been so helpful to me, but are you sure he wants to have dinner with an old woman?"

"Well, if you're old, I'm ancient. I think he'll be delighted. In fact, you fed him so many goodies when he was working in your yard he threatened to move away from my cooking and into your house," he said good-naturedly.

Roz pondered over what to fix. She wanted to make it rather special, but decided that maybe a teenage young man would prefer something like steak rather than something like salmon and salad. And of course, something chocolate.

On Saturday, Katy would be at the shop with Julia, so Roz took a day off. She bought some steaks, some very fresh vegetables and beautiful fresh red raspberries. Just what she needed for a decadent double chocolate, raspberry filled cake.

As she prepared the dinner she found her thoughts kept returning to the shop. She wondered what things she would change if it were her shop. They really had nice gift items, but the selections were small. Could it be displayed differently? Then reality set in as she remembered it was Sarah's shop, not hers. She had better concentrate on dinner. What about Mike? For almost a year now she had assumed that there was a Mrs. Mike. I wonder if he is widowed or divorced. I wonder why she'd leave him when he seemed so nice. And why had she, Roz, become so wrapped up in her own concerns that she never thought to ask before.

And then she had another thought. Almost without planning she was having dinner with a second man in a short period of time. When she ate with Will she had on jeans. Should she dress up this time? She decided to wear a long, soft print skirt with a matching top and her flat sandals. That should be casual enough.

Mike and Tim arrived bringing her a bottle of wine and a box of candy. Roz was very pleased and asked Mike to open the wine while she got a soda for Tim. She saw Tim taking in everything around the house. He went to the piano and softly placed his hands on the keys.

"Tim, do you play the piano?" she asked. "Please sit down and play something."

Tim looked over at his dad and with a smile sat down at the piano and began to play *Clair de Lune*. He played very well. It was obvious he had many lessons. She looked at Mike and saw the pride in his eyes. When he finished Mike gave his son a rub on his head and said "I guess maybe those lessons and practice sessions paid off after all. I thought we'd have to put a football on the piano to get you interested in music again."

"You just wait to hear me play after I've practiced again," Tim told his dad. Then looking at Roz he asked, "Does your daughter play the piano?"

Roz remembered that last Fourth of July when Jenny had been there. Tim and a crew had been working in the yard the day the young people had arrived. He must have heard her playing then. "Well, both Jenny and Jeff, my son, had lessons and learned enough to be able to enjoy the music but I'm afraid neither of them concentrated enough to master the keys the way you did. You're really quite good. Do you plan for a career in music?"

"Oh, I'm not that good," he said. "But sometimes I like to shake up the old man over there."

Roz could see the love between them. For a moment she felt a pang as she remembered how Rob never had time to attend even one of Jeff and Jenny's recitals. But she'd enjoyed each one no matter how long and how repetitive they got.

Roz asked Mike to cook the steaks on the grill while she

put the rest of the food on the table. The three of them had a very enjoyable meal, laughing, each one of them contributing to the conversation. Roz was beaming with all the compliments on her cooking. After finishing the meal, Tim began to clear the table but Roz stopped him.

"Are you trying to win brownie points so Rose will invite you back," Mike jokingly said to Tim.

"You got that right, Dad," said Tim. "If I don't have to do dishes is it OK if I leave now to meet the guys?" Mike said it was.

"Do you think it's too cold for coffee on the porch?" Roz asked Mike after Tim had left.

"Sounds great to me," he answered. "Let me get a jacket from the car."

The evening was beautiful with a soft breeze blowing. They sat on the swing as the darkness set in and saw that activity on the lake was beginning for the summer. There were two sailboats on the lake. The reflections of their running lights cast sparkles on the rippling water. Occasionally another boat with lights would move cross the lake.

"This has been a really pleasant evening. Thank you so much for inviting Tim and me for dinner. Two bachelors in the house cannot create the same mood that we felt here tonight," Mike said.

"I'm so glad you could come. Tim is such a nice young man. I can see that you two have a very special relationship between you."

"He's a good boy. He's not perfect. He gets into trouble on occasion but he tries hard to do the right thing. I'll certainly be lost when he goes to school next fall. It's been just the two of us for most of his life."

Roz was startled by his statement - curious to know what happened but not wanting to seem too nosy. Finally, after a couple of quiet moments, she said, "Well, I think that's a great compliment to you. Did he ever know his mother?"

"Probably not, though I like to think we kept his mother alive in his thoughts and memory. Jean was pregnant when we discovered she had breast cancer. In those days there were not many choices for treatments. She refused any treatment that might hurt the baby. Before Tim was six months old, she passed away. But she had those months to love him and create items that would make memories for him. Jean was a budding concert pianist when we got married and constantly filled the house with music. I think Tim inherited her gift for music. I started him on music lessons when he was quite small and though he loves the piano, today he's interested in so many different things. That's OK with me. This is the time of his life that he should be discovering all sorts of new things."

"You've obviously been a wonderful father to him. You should feel proud of the young man he has become," she told him.

"Well, I didn't do it alone. My mother and father moved in next door and Jean's folks lived nearby. All five of us worked together to help create a near-normal home life for him. I was trying to get my business started and many nights I was very late getting home. Then Jean's folks moved to California to be closer to their other daughter and later my folks both died. So it has been Tim and me ever since. But it's been good."

Roz and Mike sat in a comfortable silence for a few minutes, each deep into their own thoughts.

Finally, Mike said, "I'm not sure what kind of magic you wove around me tonight. I haven't talked about Jean for many years."

"Well, I think it's so nice that you can think and talk about her with such love. You two must have had something really special."

"Yes, I guess we did. But you can't live in the past. Life goes on. But enough talk about me. Tell me about you. All I know is that a beautiful lady from the city came to our little village. How did you happen to find us?"

"Don Cunningham is a good friend of my stepfather. My marriage was breaking up and I needed financial advice. When we came to see Don I felt a serenity here when I sat on his porch and looked at the lake. And the rest is history."

"Then your break-up is fairly recent. No wonder you needed time to yourself."

"I'm afraid I've rather rudely isolated myself. I guess I was feeling sorry for myself along with feeling hurt and embarrassment for not seeing the break-up coming. It all happened very suddenly."

Roz suddenly felt very embarrassed that she had opened up so much. The only other people she had opened up to were her mother and John.

Mike reached over and took her hand. They sat in a comfortable silence for a few minutes.

Mike broke the silence and said "I'm glad you found Nuna Lake. I hope we'll be good for you. I know you're good for Nuna Lake."

Then rising off the swing, Mike said, "I'd better leave. This has been the nicest evening I've had for many years. I'm so glad you asked us. Thank you for inviting us." He reached for her, gave her a quick hug and was down the steps off the porch. When he reached his car he turned to wave to her a quick goodnight.

Roz was a bit puzzled by his quick departure. She probably talked too much. No, she really said very little about her past. Well, it really was a nice evening. She went back into the house, and still hearing the echoes of the music Tim played earlier, sat down at the piano and played some of the old classics she loved.

Chapter 4

Roz settled into a new routine. Every morning she would stop in at the card shop to see if they needed help. One day she was pleased when she saw Sarah there, dressed in her usual outfit of jeans and a crisp white shirt, doing paper work and checking stock levels. Sarah was glad to see her.

"How do you like these new style jeans?" she asked. Sarah had split the seam on the leg so she could fit them over her cast. After the usual morning chitchat, Sarah said she wanted to ask a very special, very big favor of Roz.

"Because of this stupid accident I'm behind in placing my Christmas order. I usually go to the showcase in Chicago to do it. This is the final week of the show. Since I'm still on crutches, and Julia insists she has neither the knowledge nor the taste to place the order, would you go and do it for me?"

"I wouldn't know how to do that," Roz protested.

"I can tell you what to order and who to see to get help," Sarah coaxed.

"But you're putting the future of this store in my hands. I have no retail knowledge. I don't know how to do it."

"I'll be as near as your cell phone," Sarah told her.

Roz thought for a minute. Then she had a thought. "Why don't I drive you down to the show? We can get a wheelchair for you there and I'll push it. We can go down this afternoon, have dinner and rest up at a hotel and do the show tomorrow. Depending on how tired you are we can either come home or stay over a second night. We can have a girl's time out together."

Roz could see that Sarah was taken aback by such a generous offer.

"That would be fun but I can't expect you to do all that."

Julia spoke up. "Go. I'll stay here and tend the store while you're gone."

They decided to leave that afternoon.

Roz packed a small overnight bag and gathered some pillows and a blanket so Sarah could rest easier in the car. She phoned ahead to a hotel near the mart where the sales show was held. She asked for a double room that would be wheelchair accessible and asked to have a wheelchair available.

While they were traveling to the city, Sarah reviewed some catalogs and made notes on what she wanted to see at the show. As she drove, Roz realized that this would be her first visit back there since the day she moved to Nuna Lake. She wondered if she'd run into any of her old friends. It was unlikely that she would. But she also remembered her self-help list and wondered if she should at least make one phone call. If she did so, whom should she call? Maybe the next door neighbor? She also thought about Mike. The evening seemed to go so well yet it had a rather abrupt ending. Well, what did she expect? After all, she had expected him to bring his wife when she invited him. Just because he wasn't married did she expect him to make mad passionate love to her? The thought made her smile. Mad, passionate love was the last thing on her mind.

When they arrived at the hotel, the doorman greeted her with a big smile and a warm welcome.

"Mrs. Graham it's been so long. We're so glad to see you back here. Welcome."

The doorman helped Sarah into the chair and pushed the chair into the lobby. Roz was pleasantly surprised to be welcomed so warmly. For several years she had arranged the hotel's annual Christmas party as well as other parties held there. But she didn't expect them to remember her. They'd arranged a suite for her. Sarah was very pleased with all the VIP treatment but she was tired from the trip. She settled into her room and Roz decided to order room service so that Sarah could rest up for the next day.

Sarah was surprised when she saw their dinner wheeled into the room that night and again when room service brought them breakfast the next morning.

"You're certainly making it easy for me. I don't know how I'll ever pay you for all you're doing," she said.

Roz laughed and said, "It's been a long time since I could enjoy something like this. My old job was making these kinds of arrangements. I had forgotten how much I did enjoy that part of my life. I think this trip will be good for me."

The buying trip at the auditorium was a real experience for Roz, but Sarah went at it like the pro she was. She knew which sections she wanted to see and which vendors she wanted to talk with. Often she would stop when she saw something new and ask for Roz's opinion about whether or not it would be a good idea to buy it and if so, how they would display it? Roz realized that what helped Sarah's shop be a success was that she bought nothing in bulk. Never more than two or three of an item. She saw each item as unique. Before long Roz began to understand the process and began to look around on her own. She realized that Sarah was a professional businesswoman who not only had the eye for what to buy, but also kept in mind her profit margin. Sarah had many friends there and they shared many stories about their successes and their disasters of the past year.

Roz could see that Sarah was getting tired so they returned to the hotel in the late afternoon. Roz planned to order dinner in, but Sarah suggested that if they waited an hour or so, she'd like to go out for dinner if it was somewhere close to the hotel. Of course, Roz was agreeable and knew of a very nice restaurant just a few doors away.

As they made their entry into the restaurant, Roz heard a loud greeting from the bar area where people were waiting for tables. She turned to see Tom and Pat Wilson making their way to talk with her. Rob's lawyer certainly wasn't the person Roz would have chosen to see from her past but what could she do. She introduced Sarah and told them that she and Sarah were on a buying trip for Sarah's shop. Tom asked Roz about Nuna Lake. Sarah was quick to talk about Roz's perfectly beautiful new home and gardens, Sarah called it an estate, and how everyone in town loved Roz, although more and more people were calling her Rose.

As Sarah was chatting Roz looked closely at Pat. As usual, she was dressed in the latest fashion in a stylish-cut dinner suit. She had a new hair style, and sparkled with diamonds in her ears and on her fingers. A diamond brooch was on her lapel.

"Roz, you look perfectly wonderful. You look so rested and healthy and fit. Do you work out every day? How do you keep in shape?" Pat Wilson asked. For a moment Roz wanted to strike out and say a year of crying and grief does change a person. But instead she smiled and said confidently, "I have a good life." Roz paused for just a second then continued, "That's an unusual brooch you're wearing." The brooch was a star design. There was a large diamond in the center with smaller diamonds going from the center to each point of the star and a larger diamond on each point.

Pat's face paled instantly. Tom spoke up and said, "She's had that for years. It was from an old boyfriend. I guess I should be jealous….." His voice wavered as if a light bulb had just been turned on.

Pat quickly said, "Tom, find out why we're still waiting for a table."

Just then the maitre d' arrived to tell Roz and Sarah their table was ready, so they said their goodbyes.

Roz knew that Sarah must be very curious about the conversations. After they were seated Sarah said, "I shouldn't pry so don't feel compelled to explain, but did I just witness some drama back there?"

"Drama of the biggest kind." Roz paused not knowing how much to say. Then she thought I've done nothing wrong. What's wrong with sharing personal feelings with a friend?

"I just learned that my ex-husband had an affair with someone I considered a good friend."

"Oh, Roz, I'm so sorry."

"Really, Sarah, it's fine. That brooch she is wearing is one that Rob's father designed and had made special for his mother. After she died I kept it in my jewelry box. It wasn't really my style so I wore it very little. One day it disappeared. Rob told me he put it in the safety deposit box. Now I know where it went."

"Did you know he was cheating on you?"

"No. I didn't know until he left me to marry another woman just last year."

"Pat went white as a sheet when you recognized the brooch. From the look on Tom's face I think maybe he realized who gave it to her."

"I'm sure he did. Rob bragged about it all the time."

"Well, I bet Tom and Pat are having an interesting conversation about now."

The waiter arrived with the menu and they enjoyed the elegance of the restaurant and the menu. No more was said about the encounter. That night Roz thought about the incident and wondered how many other women Rob had been with during their marriage. And she wondered how she would have reacted if she had known about it.

The next day the trip home went quickly as they talked about the purchases they had made, where they would store it and how they would display it. Retailing was a whole new world for Roz and she had many questions about everything. Sarah complimented her on the sale she had made to Will.

"You are a natural at customer service," she told Roz. Then she asked, "Do you miss your life in the city? It's so different in Nuna Lake."

"This is the first I've been back since I moved last year. And, no, I don't miss it. I had an existence there and I have happy memories of my children there, but not the life I have in Nuna Lake. Maybe I had to come back for a visit to make me realize how much at home I feel in Nuna Lake."

"Well, Nuna Lake likes you. Oh course, there are a few people who think you should be married to one of our locals so you won't leave, but they are still trying to decide who would be quite classy enough for you," Sarah told her with a giggle.

"Quit teasing me, Sarah," laughed Roz, "or I'll have to sell my house and move back to the city."

"I'm not sure Mike Nelson would let you go. Now Will might follow you there. Hmmmm, I'll have to ponder on this for a while," Sarah teased.

Roz started to laugh. "And to think, it is really Harry Moore I really wanted but his wife is so nice I'll have to give him up."

"Millie is so sweet. And she has been very sick. I hear your lemon pie really hit the spot," Sarah told her.

While Sarah was resting a bit on their way home, Roz thought about their conversation. It has been years since I had a girlfriend that I could share laughs or worries with. She thought about Mike Nelson and Will Laughlin. She knew she would see both of them again but just as two good friends. That's the way she wants it.

Roz was very happy to see her own house and settle in for the evening. She checked her answering machine and saw she had two messages. She decided not to even see who had called until she had changed clothes and had a cup of herbal tea out on her porch. It was so restful there. She saw that the lake activity was busier. The leaves on the trees in her yard were almost fully in bloom. She wondered if she should have told Sarah about her past life. It had been a bit disconcerting when they had run into Tom and Pat. She thought about Rob and wondered how many other women he had in his life. She wondered about Sarah. She really knew so little about Sarah's life away from the store. I wonder if it's good or bad that I know so little about the people around me, she thought. Do I seem like a cold fish just interested in myself? I really would like to know more about everyone.

She finally went in and checked her messages. One was from her mother. "Please try to be home early this evening. We'll call back then. Everything's OK but we need to talk to you."

The second message was from Mike. "Sorry you're not there so I can apologize in person. I had a wonderful evening with you and I'm sorry I left so abruptly. I was a jerk. I have to be out of town for a couple of days but if you can, please keep Saturday evening open and let me take you out for dinner. I'll call you when I get back."

Well, that's a surprise, she thought. Then she thought about the first call. She couldn't imagine why her mother would leave a message like that. They usually communicated by e-mail. She hoped Jenny was OK.

She quickly checked her e-mail, hoping for a clue but there was nothing important there.

She was glad she didn't have to wait too long until the phone rang and she heard the voice of her daughter.

"Mom, it's me. Where were you?" Jenny asked.

"I went to Chicago on a buying trip with Sarah, my new friend. She was buying Christmas stock for her store."

"I'm glad to hear that you're making friends, Mom," Jenny said. "Tell me about it."

"Jenny, I can tell by your voice that you have some kind of news. What's going on?"

"I was going to e-mail you but Grandpa and Grandma thought I should call you about it."

"So what's going on?"

"Carrie and I made friends with a group of people working for the United Nations. They're going to Africa to do relief work and could use both of us to help them. I know you are expecting me home and if you need me, I'll come home. But if you're OK, I really would like to go with the group. It'll only be for three months. I don't need any money from you."

"What about graduation? I thought you planned to come home for the actual ceremony."

"I've already earned my credits. It's not important to me to have the ceremony right now. If I change my mind I can attend the ceremony in December. I'll only be in Africa for a short time."

"Did you talk with your dad? Did he object?" Roz asked.

"I couldn't reach him. Dad doesn't care what I do."

"What about shots, or visas, or whatever. It can't be all that simple to go to Africa."

"Mom, Africa's not the end of the world. Think of how good it'll look on my resume when I get a real job. I'm getting lonesome to see you but the trip is only for three months. If I come home first, I might never come back or have this chance again. Please say it's OK with you unless you really need me to come home."

"Jenny, I appreciate your concern and I love you so much for thinking about me. I'm doing just fine here. I've made friends and I'm keeping busy. Please don't worry about me. You're of an age now to make your own decision. Do what you think best. You're doing it with my blessing. I am anxious to see you but three months isn't very long. We'll have time to catch up later."

Roz could hear the relief in Jenny's voice when she hung up. Her little Jenny was growing up. She'd expected to hear Jenny making plans for the summer. Instead, she was planning to go to Africa to help others. That's a pretty darned good kid I got, she thought. Jenny even sounded different - older, more settled. Suddenly Roz was very lonesome to see her daughter. It would only be for three months, and then Jenny would be home. She decided to write her a quick e-mail and then call Jeff. She needed to hear his voice.

Jeff and Karen were happy to talk with her. They were excited for Jenny. But they also wanted to quiz Roz about her life. They told her they didn't get enough details in the e-mails. When she told them about her buying trip they were very interested. Karen was a buyer for a large department store company so she was very interested and actually very helpful with hints for Roz if she should ever make another buying trip. Karen asked about the type of customers the shop attracted and Roz told them about helping Will make his purchases. By the time they had talked a while, Jeff and Karen decided they should make a trip to Nuna Lake. They decided to come up in two weeks.

The next day Roz decided not to go into the store. She made a quick call to Sarah to make sure she had survived the trip and wasn't too tired and then decided to take a look in the garage.

It was dark and dirty inside. The only vacant area was the place where the swing and table had been. They had been close to the door. Roz decided to carry out anything that she could and take a better look at it. There were a lot of tools, some yard furniture, and five old lawn mowers. Five genera- tions of lawn mowers, Roz decided. There was an old croquet set as well as badminton equipment and tennis racquets in fairly good shape and a set of bocce balls. There were quite a few pieces of lawn furniture. It appeared that the owners had probably entertained a lot and wanted everyone comfortable. Most of it had been put away carefully. There were some boxes of papers but she couldn't immediately identify what they were about. She wondered what she should do with all these things. She remembered that Will had bought a gift for a local man who was a historian of local information, a man named Mr. Markham. Maybe he'd be interested in seeing at least the papers. She knew that most people would call all these things junk, but maybe they were antiques instead. The thought of anyone getting excited over old tools, etc. made her smile.

On Saturday morning the phone rang early. It was Mike.

"Good morning," he said cheerfully. "I hope you had a good trip to the city. I hope you got my message when you got home and I hope you kept tonight open for dinner with me."

"Hi, Mike. Yes, yes, and yes. I really learned a lot about merchandising, both buying and displaying. Sarah's so knowledgeable it was fun to be with her. But how did you know about it so soon if you've been out of town?"

"Rose, you must know by now that nothing goes unseen in this town. People are very nice about not nosing into your life, but trust me, people know everything," he laughed. "The news around here is kind of an unprinted newspaper. I heard about the trip by three o'clock the day you left," he went on. "But please don't be mad at anyone. They all mean well, and are really there if you need them."

"I've made a lot of friends here lately. Being away made me appreciate how much I really feel like this is my home."

"That's good news," he replied. "Now, let's talk about tonight. Can you be ready about six? I thought we'd go to The Lake House. It's a restaurant on the other side of the lake and the food may not match yours, but it's really pretty good. It'll take us about half an hour to drive over and should give us time to walk along the beach if the weather stays nice."

"That sounds wonderful; I'll see you then."

She decided to wear a long white skirt, full enough for easy walking, and an open weave light blue sweater over a matching top. When Mike smiled his approval at her appearance she knew she'd made a good choice.

As they drove to the lake, Roz told Mike about starting to clear out the garage and the five generations of lawn mowers. He became quite interested and told her there was a museum that had a section for yard and garden tools and how they have changed over the years. He thought they might be interested. She also told him there appeared to be a big desk or cabinet in the back but she had to move a few more things out before she could get to it. He told her that if she liked he would bring Tim over to help move out some of the things.

"I'd really appreciate your help. I'm not sure what many of these things are and whether or not they're worth saving."

"I'm no expert but I'll be glad to look. I'm not surprised that there were garden tools there. When I was a boy the people who lived here had a gardener who worked three days a week. The grounds were spectacular. What you're calling a garage was a very large garden shed at one time."

This was Roz's first trip around the lake and she was surprised at how big it really was. There were many curves in and out around the shoreline that weren't visible from her house. The restaurant had been there many years. It was so well kept that it looked almost new. It was a favorite place to eat for both tourists and locals. The late spring flowers were blooming along the pathway from the parking area. From the parking area there was another walk among other gardens to the beach and along the water for maybe a mile or so. There were lighted torches among the flowers to show off their beauty.

They decided to have dinner before walking. Mike was warmly greeted by the owners, Dorothy and Ed Haskins, and introduced Roz to them.

"Mrs. Graham, welcome to The Lake House," the owners said as they shook her hand. "We heard you'd moved here last summer. We're glad you're here. We hope you'll enjoy your dinner and come back often."

The restaurant was easily on a par with any of the finest restaurants in the city. The ambiance was pleasant and relaxing. They had a glass of wine as they reviewed the menu and finally decided on lake fish that had been caught that day, served with fresh vegetables. The food was excellent.

Mike talked a little about his business trip out of town. He was working with a group of botanists to develop some new hybrids of old flowers that would be better suited to the environment. He'd be getting some of them to test in this area. Roz told Mike about seeing all the gift items and how much consideration Sarah had given her purchases and what a good businesswoman she was. She decided she didn't know him well enough to tell him about the event with Pat Wilson.

It was a very pleasant meal. Mike suggested they walk the beach and then come back for dessert and coffee. It was beautiful walking along the water. The moon was rising and casting its golden glow onto the water. It felt very natural to Roz to be in this place with this man. They walked along hand in hand in a comfortable silence. They came to a large rock that jutted out into the water. Mike climbed up to the top, pulling Rose along with him. The rock was very flat on top. Mike called it the "Sitting Rock" since most everyone liked to rest a while before walking back.

They sat there quietly for a few minutes and then Mike said he wanted to explain about his quick departure from her house the week before. She started to tell him no explanation was necessary, but he said he needed to tell her.

"Most people around here know my history. They know my family, Jean's family, Tim; well I guess they just know me. I can't even remember the last time I'd mentioned Jean's name. You're so easy to talk to and it just all came out. In all the years since her death I guess I never met anyone who made me feel the way you make me feel, Rose. I feel I could tell you anything. I never expected to have feelings for anyone again. And for all these years, I hadn't. But I did feel something special with you. But those feelings also scared me a bit. I thought I probably had talked too much and I'd better quit while I was ahead. At least I hoped I was ahead." As Mike talked with her he had placed both of her hands in his. And he looked very seriously as he asked her, "Did I blow it?"

Roz looked directly into his eyes. "Mike, I'm so flattered. You definitely didn't blow it. I thought that maybe I'd blown it by what I said about me. It could be a turn-off to anyone. Mike, you're a very special person. And honestly, I think I'm just now finding out who I am."

Roz then told Mike about Rob and the children and Rob's announcement of the year before; her search for healing and self-worth, and her move to Nuna Lake. "Part of me wanted to hide away and not see anyone. I was embarrassed because I was too dumb to see it coming. I felt a lot of insecurity about making a life on my own without being dependent on my children," she told him.

"Can you talk about Rob?" he asked her. "I think he's a jerk for ever letting you go, but he must have some good points if you were in love with him."

"I guess ambitious is the word I would use for Rob. He always wants things politically correct and plans his moves carefully. We were a couple from the time we were both very young and got married long before either one of us was independent enough to make a life on our own. He had certain expectations for me. I'm trying not to be too judgmental of him because I know now I could have been stronger myself but I just kind of drifted with the tide and tried not to make waves. It was a horrid shock, but I now know it wasn't the end of my life."

They sat quietly together, just looking at the water. Then looking at him, she told him, "I never thought I would reach this point. But to talk this way helps me put him in the past.

I want more out of life than I got with Rob. The only things we had together were the children, and I love them dearly. But honestly, Mike, I just can't imagine having this kind of a conversation with him. He'd have told me to get over this silliness."

Then Mike said, "Let's move the conversation to something a little lighter. You know all about Tim. Tell me about your kids."

Roz told Mike about Jenny and her phone call of the past week. "Jenny is my outgoing, fun loving, inquisitive, daughter. Jeff is charming like his dad but a more thoughtful, sensitive man. He and his wife will be coming up next weekend. They feel a certain responsibility to see how I'm getting on with my life."

"He sounds like a good guy. Do you think I could meet him or do you want the time alone with him?"

Feeling very content with her life at that moment she told him she would like for them to meet.

He gently pulled her to her feet, put his arms around her and first kissed her lightly, and then as their feelings took over, they kissed passionately, both with a hungry desire. They pulled away slowly, both of them trying to deal with feelings that had long been missing from both their lives, and walked back up the beach.

As she got ready for bed that night she thought about how she felt when Mike took her in his arms. She wondered if she had ever felt that way before. She liked that feeling and knew she wanted to feel that way again. But would she ever have the opportunity with Mike? She took a long look at her body in the mirror. Rob had always told her that her breasts were too small and her stomach was too big; that she needed to exercise more to give her arms and legs more shape. Roz had not had the courage to defend herself. She tried to pretend it didn't hurt her when he said such things. Now she took a new look at her body. It wasn't great but she didn't think she looked too disgraceful. She could see some cellulite on her legs and a bit of flab around her belly but considering her age she guessed it wasn't too bad. But would she want anyone else looking at her body? Had the shape of her body driven Rob away? No, she thought. He left me a long time before he walked out the door. Probably years ago. I just didn't realize it. She looked again at her breasts. They still looked pretty firm and didn't sag much. She had a sudden thought that she hadn't had her mammogram last year or this. Maybe she'd call for an exam next week.

That night she laid in bed she tried to sort out her feelings. These were feelings she couldn't remember ever having before. Mike made her feel so good, so important, so worthy of a better life. Feeling this way, could she ever be content to just be good friends with him? She was afraid she couldn't. But she also felt that Mike might never be ready to take the next step to the future. He had a good life, one that had satisfied him. A good friend might be all he needs, she thought. If I can't be satisfied with that would it be better not to have any relationship? Can I survive the risk of being rejected again?

After a night of tossing and turning, she finally decided to take one day at a time and try to enjoy not only a friendship with Mike, but also with all the other people of Nuna Lake who were so good to her.

Mike and Tim came by the next morning and were quite impressed to see her collection of tools in such good shape. "It looks like the gardener kept all his tools here," Mike told her.

Tim was pushing his way past the furniture and suddenly yelled out, "Hey, Rosie, there's a canoe back here. Come help me move stuff, Dad."

Together, Mike and Tim moved things and unearthed a beautiful old canoe. But Roz was more impressed with the old roll top desk that could now be seen. Under the grime she could see the beautiful wood and all the little drawers and nooks in it. What a gem, she thought.

Tim looked at Roz empathetically and said, "Rosie, if you move out all this junk and the desk and this wonderful canoe, you might actually be able to park your car in there in the winter. Isn't that a clever idea," he said, dramatically throwing his hands in the air. "Just imagine a car in a garage. What a unique idea." He was so serious as he said it they had to laugh.

Roz told Mike she would make a list of all the items that she wanted taken out of there. It would be nice if they could go to a museum. She would call Mr. Markham to see if he knew of a home for anything else. If all else failed, they would go to the trash.

"Let's just leave everything on the porch except for the canoe and desk," Roz suggested. "There'll be plenty of time to dispose of them."

After Mike and Tim left, Roz was pleasantly surprised when she received a call from Sarah inviting her for dinner that night. Sarah's mother was in town and was cooking a roasted chicken and they wanted to say thank you to Roz for all her help. Roz graciously accepted. She cut a bouquet of flowers to take to Sarah. It was a very relaxed dinner with friendly conversation. She learned Sarah had a business degree and her goal in life had always been to own her own shop. She had a very long time romance with Bob Johnson, a man who loved big city life and wanted Sarah to join him in Atlanta. Sarah loved her home, loved her shop and was content to be where she was.

"I don't want to be selfish, but I don't think I could ever be content in Atlanta," she told Roz. "I think I'd like to have a family someday, but I see that family growing up here in Nuna Lake. Not Atlanta, at least not yet. And maybe never. It's the thing we argue about the most."

"I think you're wise to take your time, no matter how long it takes," Roz told Sarah. "Sometimes I think Rob and I got married just because it was the thing our friends were doing. I don't regret it because we have two wonderful kids. I expected it to last forever. It didn't and it was an unexpected shock when he told me he was leaving. I wasn't sure I would ever have a life again. And then I came to Nuna Lake. Its taken time to get over it but I now feel I have a whole new life ahead of me. And one I'm looking forward to living."

"And Nuna Lake's glad to have you here," Sarah told her. "When you didn't come into the shop the past few days, I thought I'd lose some sales. One customer is coming back to buy a vase next week. She wants to talk with you about which shape to buy. I don't know how in the world I can ever thank you for all your help. You won't let me pay you. There must be something I can do."

"It's been fun for me," Roz said. "And I'm sure I'll think of something......yes, I just have. My daughter-in-law is coming to visit this weekend. I'd like to bring her to the store to meet you. She's a buyer for a department store. She was so interested when I told her about your shop and our trip to the city."

"I'd love to meet her. Julia and I both are working that day. It's prom day for Katy. It'll be fun showing off my shop. She might even have some great ideas on how we can make changes to increase business. She's younger than me so I bet she has some great up to date ideas"

"Sarah, last night I remembered that I haven't had a mammogram for almost two years. I suppose I should really get one. Do you have a doctor you can recommend?"

"Sure, call Dr. Alex Forton. The clinic is down the street from the shop. He's great. Lucy's his nurse. Just give her a call and she'll make the arrangements."

When she got home Roz got a call from Judy Martin.

"There are a few of us who volunteer at the women's shelter over in Sprucedale. It's not too far away for women from Nuna Lake to go to if they have a need. But the place is rather small and dingy. We know we can't do too much to change it but we'd like to at least try to brighten it up. We wondered if you'd have time to join us for a brainstorming session to see what ideas we can come up with. We need someone with fresh ideas and a new look at the place."

"Well, I've never done anything like that before so I'm not sure I could contribute very much. When are you meeting?" Roz asked.

"On Wednesday around noon at my house. I'll provide the lunch and you bring some ideas," Judy answered, sounding very pleased that Roz would join them.

Roz sat by the phone thinking about the phone call. She certainly had heard of women's shelters, but she really knew nothing about them. She didn't think she could contribute anything but she could identify with being faced with having to make changes. She recognized that as painful as her experience had been, she had it so much easier than most women. She didn't have the money worries, and even if she had no money, she had a part time job then and the skills to go full time. Her children were grown. She had not been physically abused. As Roz began to think about it she realized she had been emotionally and definitely verbally abused. During her marriage she realized that she had learned not to make Rob angry by keeping her mouth shut. A good marriage is more than that. She thought about her mother. Ann had two good marriages; first with Roz's father before he died, and then with John. Their marriage was built on mutual respect and love.

As she sat there deep in thought the phone rang again. This time she heard the cheerful voice of Jeff.

"Hi, Mom. We're sure looking forward to our trip up this weekend."

"I'm so glad you are coming. I'm looking forward to seeing you again. It 's been so long I'm afraid you will have grown some more and I won't know you anymore," Roz playfully answered.

"Yea, I'm still a growing kid. Will you make me some clothes that fit?"

"Anytime, Jeff, anytime."

"Dear, sweet beautiful Mother of Mine........," Jeff began.

"Okay, Jeff. What do you want?"

"I have a favor to ask of you. Do you think you could arrange for me to meet with Don Cunningham or would that be imposing on him? I'm facing some changes here at the bank and have an opportunity to form a partnership with a group. I'm feeling very unsure about it all and would like to talk with someone who has experience in the area. I thought of Don."

"Of course. I've been trying to say thank you to some of the people who have been so helpful to me. And he certainly was. Why don't I invite Don and Beth for Sunday Brunch? You could meet him then."

"Great. Karen says she can't wait to come up and sit on the porch. So we'll see you late on Friday."

Roz decided to call Beth right away.

"Roz, dear. How very nice to hear from you. I hear you've been quite busy these days helping out Sarah so much. That's so nice of you," Beth said. "How are things going for you? Are you settled in? Are you learning to be happy again? I felt bad that we were away for the winter and couldn't be of help to you."

By this time Roz had learned that although the people of Nuna Lake would never confront someone with what they knew, nothing anyone did passed unnoticed. Roz was beginning to like that.

"Beth, it was a hard year. The move here went well and everyone was so pleasant to me, but I hid away for most of the time. One day when I woke up I realized the past was behind me and it was time to move on. I've been more social in the last month than I was for the previous twelve months. Actually, that's why I'm calling now. Jeff and Karen are coming up for the weekend and I want to invite you and Don for Sunday brunch. Is this too late a notice?"

"Of course not," Beth replied. "It'll be so good to see Jeff and Karen. I don't believe we've seen them since their wedding.

What's he doing now? Is he still at the bank? I have a feeling Don would like some bank talk."

"Actually, Beth, Jeff would like to talk with Don. I told him I was going to invite you and Don to say thanks for all your help and support. I have so many people to thank. Jeff said he thought of Don when he wondered who he could turn to for career advice. It sounds to me like he might be planning a career change."

"We'll be happy to see you all. We're planning a trip to London next month and plan to see John and Ann. I know they'll want a report about how you're doing. It'll be great to have first hand knowledge."

Late that night the phone rang as she was preparing for bed.

"Hope it's not too late to call," came Mike's voice. "I just wanted to tell you that I really enjoyed having dinner with you last night. It was a special evening for me."

"It was special for me too, Mike." Roz felt that she wanted to say more but wasn't sure if she should really open up. There really hadn't been time that morning when Tim had been with them to tell Mike how special the evening before had been for her. "I had almost forgotten how much fun it is to have friends and family around. My social events of the last few years have been times of being socially correct, you know, saying the right things, speaking to everyone. Trying to be the person everyone expected me to be. It was a kind of a sham as I think about it. You let me be me. Thank you for that."

"Why would anyone ever want you to be something other than yourself? Don't ever change who you are. Not for me. Not for anyone. I hope you'll always be the same wonderful person you are."

"You're much too nice. And it feels good to be accepted as I am. Do you have a busy week planned?"

He updated her on his work and asked about her week. She told him about her upcoming committee meeting. He told her he knew of the work of these women and they really were trying to help the women in need. He told her to let him know if they needed money for their projects. She told him about Jeff's call and about wanting to meet with Don Cunningham. Then, as she talked she remembered about the Sunday brunch she was planning.

"You said you'd like to meet Jeff. Could you and Tim stop by and join our brunch on Sunday? If the day is warm we'll eat out on the patio and you can enjoy the beauty you have created around here."

"Yes, I'd like that."

As she hung up the phone she thought of the pleasant conversations they had. She felt she could totally be herself when she talked with him. She remembered how she usually planned out her conversations with Rob ahead of time so she wouldn't upset him.

Roz thought about her evening before and how full this day had been. Mike and Tim stopping by. Going to Sarah's for dinner. Her phone calls from Jeff, her chat with Beth, and a new project to be interested in at the shelter. It really felt good to end it all with a talk with Mike. I really am making a new life here, she thought.

Roz wasn't quite sure what to wear when she was getting ready to go to Judy's. Should she wear a skirt? Or slacks? Or even jeans? She wasn't sure who the other women were who would be there. She started to feel a bit uneasy until she remembered that particular feeling as one she always had when she'd go out with Rob. He usually told her what to wear. No more, she thought. You don't have control over me, Rob. You are gone. She reached for her jeans and a white shirt. That's something she'd wear if she were going to Sarah's. She felt good and knew it would be OK. Judy's home was lovely and she had a delicious luncheon: turkey, walnut, cranberry salad, and a sinfully rich torte. There were six other women there, all wearing jeans. After the first ten minutes, Roz felt like she was one of them, laughing, chatting, and having fun as they ate lunch. She learned that there was one other member who was not there. Clair, a psychologist, was working that day.

When Roz asked them what they do at the shelter, she was told they do anything they are asked to do, make up clean rooms, sort donated items, clean the kitchen, stuff envelopes to solicit donations, or anything else. Two of them try to go each week. Clair volunteered time each week to talk with the guests as the group called them if there was a need. Judy recalled one time when she played with the children so Clair could have time alone with the mother.

These women felt the place needed some sprucing up. Maybe some paint for the rooms in a more cheerful color. Or maybe try to fix up a room with toys for the children. They were very serious about their undertaking, trying to figure out what it would cost for each of their ideas. When they were satisfied they had enough of a range of ideas along with their idea of the costs, they decided to present the list to the manager to get her priorities. Roz asked how they paid for their projects and was told that this was the first time they would be planning anything that involved money. Judy volunteered to ask the local merchants for donations once they knew how much they would need. Another volunteer, Diane, said she would check out actual costs to see if their projections were close. Altogether, it seemed a doable task.

Chapter 5

Roz spent Friday morning getting groceries and making up the guestroom for Jeff and Karen. She stopped in at Sarah's to confirm that it was still OK for her to bring Karen in the next afternoon. Roz realized that she missed being at the shop when she saw a few things had been moved around. When a customer came in looking for a gift, Roz took time to help her. Sarah laughed as she rang up the sale and told Roz she'd better watch out or retailing might get in her blood.

Jeff and Karen arrived around eight o'clock that evening. After hugs and smiles all around, Roz led them to the kitchen for a light meal. They took their coffee out to the front porch to sit and relax. Jeff and Karen were impressed with the beauty of the yard and how much work had been done in it since their last visit.

"Wait till daylight and you will see more. The rose garden is just starting to bloom and it is beautiful," she told them.

Karen was most anxious to talk about Roz's retailing experiences, and Roz loved talking about it. Jeff was very interested in the boats on the lake, asking her if she planned to learn to sail. She told him, no, but that she did have a canoe in the garage. There was no electricity in the garage so Jeff took a big flashlight to check out the canoe.

"Maybe I should put it in the lake tomorrow and try it out." he said when he returned.

"Maybe you should check it out tomorrow to see if it's full of holes," she told him.

She told him about the other tools, most of which were on the porch, around the corner of the house. And the boxes of papers she had not yet looked at.

"What'll you do with all the tools and lawnmowers," he asked.

She told him that Mike possibly knew of a museum that might be interested. But if he, Jeff, wanted anything, he had first choice.

"Well," Jeff said, "I'll let him have the lawn mowers but I might want the canoe. Don't you think that is just what we need, Karen?" he asked.

"Yes," said Karen. "You can paddle it down the city streets every time it rains."

Jeff retorted back, "Laugh, you silly woman. But you'll be glad we have a canoe when the floods hit our city street."

Roz was so happy to see the good-natured ribbing going on between them: the way that they looked at each other and apparently supported each other. As Jeff talked about his job concerns, Karen was very much a part of the conversation, making suggestions about things he should consider, and there to support and encourage him if he should decide to make a move.

As Roz tidied up the kitchen after they had gone to bed, she realized how much she missed having the family around. She especially missed Jenny tonight. She said a quiet prayer that God would watch out for Jenny and that Jeff and Karen would always be there for each other through good times and bad.

The next morning after breakfast, Jeff and Karen wanted

to walk the estate, as they called it. As they walked along flagstone paths they could see gardens of various colors against the backdrop of large flowering bushes that led into the woods. One garden with its cosmos, snapdragons and other flowers was designed to attract birds. A birdbath was there and they could see the hummingbirds and the finches enjoying their habitat. Nearby was a large maple tree with a bench underneath so that one could sit and enjoy the birds. The rose garden with the green lawn all around it had a little bench placed so that you could rest while you enjoyed the fragrance of the roses. In the back corner of the gardens, there was a Japanese garden with a waterfall in a secluded area. There was a cutting garden with marigolds, zinnias, dianthus, and other flowers. In the fall the asters and chrysanthemums would be blooming there. There was a beautiful garden of lilies, both the big day lilies that only bloom for a day and the Stella D'Oro lilies that provided constant color. Some of the paths were lined with border flowers like impatiens and begonias and periwinkles. And many petunias. Throughout the lawn, large flowerpots filled with bright red geraniums were placed near more benches. Honeysuckle vines had been planted on a trellis near the front of the house so that you could smell their delightful fragrance when you sat on the porch in the evening. In the back where the spring bulb garden had bloomed was an all white fragrance garden; taller white pricky poppies, shiny white sun drops, and sweet alyssum mixed with airy baby breath. A trellis of white moonflowers was placed at the back of the patio. Jeff and Karen were very impressed.

"This property really looks spectacular." Karen said. "It's a welcoming friendly place. I could sit here for hours." Jeff added, "Mike Nelson really knows his stuff. This property really looks like something in a magazine. Remember all the brush and weeds that were here last summer?"

"I'd like to meet Mike and ask him why my houseplants die," Karen said. "I guess I have a purple thumb."

"As a matter of fact you'll get a chance to meet him. He and Tim, his son, will be here for brunch," Roz told them.

Roz noticed that Jeff and Karen exchanged a brief look but no comments were made.

They returned to the house to find the phone ringing. It was Don Cunningham calling to talk to Jeff. Roz and Karen fixed coffee and took it to the front porch. Jeff soon joined them

"I don't know what you said to him, Mom, but he was so nice. He suggested we meet for lunch. He said he'd enjoy hearing what's new in banking. He made me feel like I would be doing him a favor instead of intruding. I hope it's OK that I said yes."

"Of course it's OK. Karen and I are going to Sarah's. I want to show her the shop. We can meet up again later in the afternoon.

As the bell rang announcing the arrival of Roz and Karen at Sarah's Card and Gift Shop, Sarah, without the help of her cane or walker, and Julia came forward to meet Karen. Julia had prepared a plate of cookies and she had tea and coffee ready. They sat in the back room after a quick tour of the front. When a customer came in, Roz immediately got up to help the customer as the others sat there talking. When she came back she told them about selling a cut-glass vase and how pleased the customer was to find it.

"See why everyone here loves Roz so much," Sarah asked Karen. "She's such a lady. The customers love her."

"I never thought that my mother-in-law would get interested in retailing. It's good for you, Mom. Nuna Lake is good for you. I don't think I have ever seen you look so healthy and content. Maybe we didn't realize how much pressure you had been under."

Roz did feel very content in her new world. She half-listened to the conversation between Karen and Sarah. It sounded so good to hear people be nice to each other.

"I'm really impressed with how you display your items. It's so tastefully done. You have a real talent for presenting merchandise," Roz heard Karen say.

"Well, I try to be creative. I have such a small place to show them."

"You have a good eye for buying the right pieces to fit your space. Your shop has such a classic look to it. No wonder my mother-in-law is so enthused about it."

While she heard part of the conversation Roz's mind was on the shop. "Why don't we put out that Limoge plate that came in yesterday?" Rose started to look for it.

"My mother-in-law in retailing?" Karen put her hands on her hips and turned her head in mock surprise. "I don't believe it."

"Rose, did you tell Karen how you saved my life?" Sarah asked..

"Don't be ridiculous," Rose said. "I did no such thing. I don't think I know what you're talking about."

Sarah related the story about breaking her ankle. Rose rolled her eyes as if Sarah was making it all up.

"Mom, you didn't tell us that part of it. But I'm glad you did it. It's really good to see you doing these things. Jeff and I were so worried you'd be lonely away from the city. I must admit. I've never seen you look better. I'm glad you made this move."

After visiting there a while, Rose decided to show Karen the rest of their small business district. Everywhere they stopped, people came forward to meet Rose's family. It was clear that in spite of being so isolated the past year, the community had taken her in as one of their own. Everyone commented on how the old Hick's property, the name of the original owner of Rose's house, was being restored into a beautiful home with beautiful gardens.

Jeff met them a little later for dinner in town. He was excited and bubbling with information from his visit with Don Cunningham.

"I don't know what I'm going to do yet," he told them, "but I know the questions I need to ask and the information I need to get before I make my decision. That man has more knowledge than I will ever have," he said.

"Jeff, stop that kind of talk," Karen told him. "You're so smart and you know so much already. I know you'll make the right decision."

"Now you know why I love her," Jeff told his mom as he gave his wife a hug.

The next morning as they made their way downstairs, Jeff asked what was on the menu for brunch.

"I thought I'd make a quiche, have a fruit tray and some pastries," Rose said.

"What? I don't get some of my mother's blueberry pancakes?" Jeff asked. "I make a mean omelet. I'll fix omelets for everyone if you will make me some pancakes."

"Okay, then, let's change the menu."

Rose started to get things ready for pancakes, Karen fixed a fruit tray and Jeff cut up the vegetables he would use in his omelets. It felt good to have a happy home as they laughed and worked together. By the time they got the table set and the coffee made, the Cunningham's arrived. Rose took Beth on a tour of the house and then Karen took Beth and Don on a tour of the gardens.

When the doorbell rang Rose went to the door to greet Mike and Tim. Jeff stepped away from the food preparation and held out his hand.

"Hi. I'm Jeff you must be Mike and you must be Tim," he said. "Thank you for helping my mom to have such a beautiful place to live."

"I'm glad you approve," Mike told him and then looked up as Karen and the Cunningham's came into the kitchen.

"Mike, dear," said Beth. "It's so good to see you." Don

quickly added, "I don't believe I have never seen this property look so good." Karen was introduced.

Rose passed around a tray of mimosas while they chatted briefly and then Jeff announced that he was head chef for the day and what kind of omelets did they want. While they were getting the food on the table Beth turned to Rose and said, "Tim played a Chopin piece a couple of years ago at a community program. It was magnificent. Do you still play?" she asked Tim.

"Not as much as before," he told her.

"Tim, why don't you play it for us now," Rose asked him.

Tim went to the piano and played the number perfectly. They all stopped to listen and when he was done they gave him loud cheers of "bravo!" Tim looked a bit embarrassed at all the fuss and appeared glad that it was time to eat.

While they sat around the table having a last cup of coffee, Karen commented on the beauty of the lake and its unusual name.

"Nuna Lake. What does it mean? Is it an Indian name?" she asked.

Don looked at Mike and said "I believe it's a Cherokee name, isn't it, Mike?"

"Yes," Mike answered. "There was a small tribe of Cherokees who came to this area a couple of hundred years ago. They were very taken with all the spruce trees and the big body of water. They called it *Nuna GaDaWaHi*, which means spruce trees and big water. For many years that's how it was known. When the city folks began to come here in the summer, they felt the name was too long so changed it to Nuna Lake. The local lore is that an Indian maiden and her lover drowned in the lake and when the moon casts a glow across the water, it's a path to their ancestors in the sky. It's said that there are still Indian relics buried in the area and there is an old Indian burial ground up in the hills."

Tim added, "But all we ever found were a few arrowheads."

"Tim, did you see the canoe in the garage? Do you think it might be authentic Indian?" Jeff asked him.

"I got a quick look at it when we were moving boxes out. Is there a way to tell if it's a real Indian canoe?"

Jeff asked, "Does anyone here know how to tell?"

The men then decided they had better go check it out. And, of course, they needed to check out all the tools and lawnmowers on the side porch.

The women sat chatting and Rose asked Beth about her upcoming trip to London. "Be sure to tell my mother about how well I'm doing when you see her."

"You do have a glow of contentment about you," Beth told Rose.

"I think I'm probably more content here than any time in my life, except I miss having my children closer to me. Jenny's in Africa and it's a big trip for Karen and Jeff to come so far," Rose said.

"Beth, I told Mom I hope Jeff won't make a pest of himself calling your husband," Karen told her. "He seems to feel so much better about making a decision now."

"We're glad we can help. Don has times of really missing his work. He likes to be updated about what's going on in the banking world. He was very pleased that Jeff wanted to talk with him."

When the men came back from the garage, Tim and Jeff were especially excited about restoring the old canoe. But the guests tactfully made their way home so that Roz would have a few minutes alone with Jeff and Karen before they left.

"Mom," Karen said, "I think this has been one of the nicest weekends we've had for a long time. I know I want to come back soon and often."

"Me, too," said Jeff. "Don was so helpful to me. And Tim

is quite a guy. Did you know he's planning to go to Stanford next year?"

"No, I didn't," Roz replied. "I guess I'm still not reaching out enough to other people. I'm always afraid people will think I'm being nosy."

"Well, work on it, Mom." Then Jeff went on, a little hesitant at first. "Mike is one nice guy and everyone can see he is falling for you, Mom."

"Jeff," Roz began, not quite ready to talk about Mike with her children.

But Jeff cut her off. "Don't say anything to me about it yet. But don't be afraid to reach out and take the good things life can give you. Not every man is the jerk who fathered me. You're entitled to lots of happiness. That's what I want for you."

Roz felt almost weepy as she told them goodbye. But she knew it was a good weekend. Life is being good to me, she thought.

Roz realized she had a busy week ahead after they left. She had told Sarah she would start working on a plan for displaying the Christmas items that would be shipped in August. She also planned to work at the store one afternoon. And this would be the week she had her first trip to the women's shelter. She wanted to make a list of the tools and make and model of the lawn mowers for Mike. She needed to shop for a graduation gift for Tim. She wanted to send a *care* package to Jenny. She needed to have a long talk with her mother. And she needed to say thank you to another name on her list. Oh, yes, she must remember to call the office of Dr. Forton to set up a mammogram.

As she sat on the porch with her coffee the next morning, she suddenly felt the desire to talk to Mike. Why not, she wondered? She just felt a need to hear his voice. He's probably at work she thought, so she called him there. She decided against using his cell phone number. He might be in a meeting.

His secretary answered the phone and Roz identified herself. "He's out of the office right now, but I'll page him and have him call you right back," the secretary said.

Rose told her it wasn't necessary, that she'd call back later. But almost immediately the phone rang. "Rose, is everything OK?" Mike asked anxiously.

Rose decided to be honest with Mike and said, "I just wanted to hear your voice. I wanted to make sure you and Tim survived yesterday. I hope I didn't interrupt anything important."

"This is the nicest surprise you could give me. Both Tim and I had a great visit. You have a wonderful son and daughter-in-law."

"They think you are a special person. I do too."

"Well, that is encouraging to hear. Do you have a busy day planned?"

She told him her schedule and he told her about his projects for the day. They agreed they would talk again that evening.

As she made her way to get dressed the phone rang with an urgent call from Clair.

"Rose, I know that maybe I shouldn't be calling you so quickly since you are new to the group, but I have a problem. A woman with three children was brought in to the shelter last night. I feel it's urgent that I talk with her immediately but the shelter has no one to look after the kids while I do. Is it possible for you to get away right now and help me out?"

"Of course. Where shall I meet you?"

"I'll pick you up in fifteen minutes," Clair told her.

"The story is sad but very usual," Clair told her as they drove to the shelter. "This woman was beaten so badly she should be in the hospital but refused to stay because of the kids. She didn't want to leave them with strangers. Be prepared for what you are about to see. And the kids. Most usually they're either terribly withdrawn or acting out in a bad way.

We can't tell her what to do but hopefully she won't feel she has to go back to the house where it will happen all over again. She drove herself to the hospital even though she was bleeding badly. No one knows where her abuser is now. He seems to have disappeared."

The shelter was located about ten miles from Nuna Lake. At one time the building had been a nursing home. Both the outside and inside showed their age, but even so, it was a safe haven for those who needed one. Clair introduced Rose to the manager and they made their way to the room where the family had spent the night.

Rose saw three worried children, a boy about seven, a girl about four or five and a toddler. They were clinging to their mother. Rose walked over to them and said, "Hi, my name is Rose. What's your name?"

The older boy glared at her and said nothing but the little girl said, "Patsy."

"And who is this," Rose asked looking at the toddler. "That's Joe," Patsy told her.

Clair walked over to the children and told them, "My name is Clair. I want to talk to your momma. We're going to go across the hall and close the door so we can talk. But if you want to see her, you can peek in the window and see both of us. Rose will stay here with you."

Rose wanted to cry for them all. The woman was so badly bruised and battered with stitches all over her face and arms. Rose wondered about the injuries she could not see. And to think, the children witnessed it all. Her heart ached for them. But she kept a smile on her face and picked up a stuffed animal that had been given to them by the police.

"Who is your friend?" she asked as a way of breaking the ice. And somehow she managed to keep them entertained for nearly an hour. She finally made friends with Jack, the seven-year-old, on a somewhat limited basis. He was very worried about where his mother was and really clung to his mom when she and Clair returned.

On the drive home, Clair complimented Rose on her approach with the kids.

"Does it ever get easier, working with these women?" Rose asked Clair.

"I wouldn't say it gets easier," Clair told her. "With some of them you go through it so many times. They're always sure it will never happen again. You know the drill.....He promises he won't do it again. But sometimes we do have a real success story. It's what keeps us going. We're pretty limited in what we can do. Usually, the woman already knows what she should do. She just needs someone to say the words."

"What will happen to this family?"

"She has parents who'll help her. We talked with them on the phone and they'll be driving in today to get her. Hopefully, the boyfriend will stay away."

"Do you think they're in physical danger?"

"We can never be sure but we do the best we can. Sometimes we feel like we have really gotten through but with others we know they'll be back again. Usually, the physical abuse heals more quickly than the verbal and emotional abuse. You are so ugly....you are so stupid....you are too fat, etc. It destroys many women. The woman usually feels she didn't try hard enough."

That is me to a T, Rose suddenly realized. I always thought Rob would love me more if I tried harder. It really wasn't my fault for not trying hard enough. It was a guilt trip I let him lay on me.

As Rose got out of the car at her home, Clair again thanked her for going. "Not everyone can work with the family. But you were great. I'll try not to bother you too often," she said with a smile as she drove off.

Rose spent the rest of the day in her gardens, pulling a few weeds and deadheading the flowers. She decided to inventory the lawn tools on her porch. She typed up the information to give to Mike when she saw him. Then, still feeling ambitious, she decided to bake cookies to take to Lois at the library and maybe even Millie the next day. As she was taking them out of the oven, she was very pleased when she heard Mike call her name asking if it was OK to walk in.

"I could smell something very good as I was driving by and I thought I'd better check it out," he said with a smile.

"You're just in time but you can't have any until you eat your dinner. Do you and Tim have plans for tonight?"

"Tim's with his friends tonight."

"Then why don't I fix us some pasta and then you can have a cookie."

"Wonderful. What can I do to help?" he asked.

"You make a salad and I'll cook the pasta."

In no time at all the food was ready. They carried it out to the patio. Mike told Roz about his day at work and Rose told Mike about her trip to the women's shelter.

Mike looked at Rose and said, "It's so nice to have someone to talk with. I try not to overburden Tim with work talk. After all, he is working for the family firm. So we keep it to father/son things," he said.

"Well," Rose told him, "I have never talked about my day to anyone, except perhaps my mother on occasion. Rob wasn't a bit interested in my career or my life."

"Well that was his loss. You have such an interesting variety in your life. I like hearing about your day."

After Mike left that night Rose thought about their conversation. Rob would never want to hear about abused women. In fact he would have forbidden her to go to the shelter. He would have approved of her raising funds for it, but never to go near it. Why, she wondered, did she not insist on making her own way instead of always following one step behind him. She was an intelligent, educated woman. She had to admit she never had any great inspiration to have a major career. Instead, to please Rob she had imitated Rob's mother, a woman who never quite succeeded at anything but was always trying. In some ways it was a very childlike pattern. I wonder why I was satisfied to live that way, she thought. And why did the words *forbid me* come to mind. I'm an adult. Is that the way I was living my life?

The next morning Rose felt very happy when Mike called to say good morning before he left for work. With a smile on her face Roz fixed a basket of cookies for Lois at the library and one for Millie Moore. She cut a mixed bouquet of flowers for each of them and started off on her rounds.

"Lois, this is a little thank you. You have been so nice about saving the new books for me. You made me feel welcome in this town, even if I wasn't always friendly."

"Mrs. Graham, you didn't need to do this but it is a wonderful surprise. Thank you so much. It is a pleasure to have a friend who enjoys and appreciates reading a good book."

"Please call me Roz or Rose. I seem to be getting Rose more in Nuna Lake," Roz told her.

"Actually, I do think more people in town are referring to you as Rose. Harry Moore stopped in to pick up books for Millie yesterday. He referred to you as Rose not Roz. And you know this town, everybody knows everything." she said with a smile.

Her next stop was at the hardware store to talk to Harry Moore. He was very pleased to see her. She asked him if Millie would be up to having company that day and he told her Millie would be delighted. She got directions to his house and was there very quickly. Millie was waiting on the front porch.

"You must be Rose," Millie greeted her. "Harry phoned and said you were on your way. Oh, what beautiful flowers," she said as Rose handed her the bouquet and basket of cookies. "I just made a fresh pot of coffee. Can you stay long enough so we can have it with one of these cookies?"

Rose said she did have time if Millie would let her go inside and get the coffee. Millie agreed. Millie had some obvious signs of weakness but a smile and a manner that would make anyone feel special. As Rose made her way to the kitchen she saw the house was one that looked so comfortable you wanted to sink into the chairs and stay a while.

As they chatted over coffee Millie asked Rose about her children. Then Rose asked Millie about her children and her life in Nuna Lake. Millie and Harry had met during WWII before he shipped out to the Pacific. That was nearly sixty years ago. Harry was only eighteen. They fell in love and were married immediately. When he came home, they moved to Nuna Lake where Harry's dad ran the hardware store. Harry became the sole owner when his father died.

Rose felt like she wanted to ask Millie all sorts of questions....about building a marriage of so many years.....about her decision to marry so quickly.....about any regrets, or did she have any? Soon it appeared to Rose that Millie was getting a little tired, so she told Mille she would clean up their cups and be leaving. Millie admitted she was getting a little tired and would Rose walk her to her bedroom.

"My Harry is right. You are a lady, a sweet kind woman. Thank you so much for taking time to visit me today," Millie said.

"Millie, you're such an interesting person. I look forward to visiting you again."

Later that evening Tim came to the door calling her name. "Dad and I are going to get an ice cream cone over at the Merry-Go-Round. Do you have time to go with us?"

"That sounds like fun," she said and walked to the car to join them.

"I have some good news about the lawn mowers and tools. I called GreenMower. They make the lawn mowers my staff uses. I explained I was a landscaper and I had come across these items and did they have any interest in seeing them? They said they certainly did and were most anxious to see them. They are planning an anniversary celebration for the company and think it would be good publicity to show how long lawn mowers have been around. They said they'd call me back with a date in the very near future. So maybe you will find a home for them."

Tim spoke up. "I hope you get a very good price for them."

Rose began to laugh. "I don't expect to get any money for them. I really thought I'd just throw them out but it might be nice to donate them to someone."

"Maybe GreenMower will buy them," Tim said. "If they don't want them could I try selling them on e-Bay?"

"You certainly may and you may keep whatever you can get," she told him.

"It was really fun talking with Jeff. He's a very smart guy. He asked me to help him restore the canoe. He wants to get it in the water this summer. Do you think he will be up on the Fourth of July?" Tim asked.

"Why don't I call him and invite him? Sometimes they go to New York to visit Karen's family. But it would be fun to have him here," she responded.

"Rose, you'll come with us to my graduation Saturday morning won't you?" asked Tim.

"Well, of course. Thank you for asking. It's OK with you, isn't it Mike?"

"We both want you there," Mike answered.

She called Jeff when she got home and found they were planning to be in New York on the Fourth of July. But they might come up the weekend before then. Like Tim, Jeff was anxious to get the canoe in the water.

"Do you think Tim would help me launch it?"

"I think he'd be thrilled to help you work on it," Rose told him.

She sat outside in the quiet evening and thought about her day and her life in Nuna Lake. Some of the things she was doing these days were the things her mother had done when Rose was growing up. She could remember her mother taking food to sick neighbors. She remembered family dinners. She remembered going out for ice cream cones on hot summer evenings. Just little things, but things that made you feel safe and content. When did her life start to change? At first, she and Rob had done little things together, like a walk in the park. But then Rob was always too busy. He didn't approve of so many things. One time when she had decided to take soup to a neighbor he had told her that her soup lacked pizzazz and she had better not do it.

He looked at her job as a little time-filling game because she couldn't find anything better to do. He had no idea how much time and work was involved in planning events. Often she would just be given a date and a general idea of the number of people who would attend. First she had to find a place the right size for the crowd with safe lighted parking or even valet parking. Maybe they wanted to have music or dance which meant open areas and sound systems. She had to arrange a menu which might be buffet or a sit-down dinner. If it was sit-down she would have to plan two entrees. There always would be someone with an allergy or religious restriction. If it was buffet she had to be certain to have enough variety to cover that possibility. There were details like flowers or centerpieces. Sometimes they wanted gift items for each guest. All this had to be done within a budget. She wondered if he had ever given any thought or thanks to the people who had arranged all the big events where he spent so much time trying to curry clients or relationships for future sales. The goals that Rob set for them were always uppermost in his mind. Was I really happy then living with Rob's restrictions? Or am I happier now, even living alone?

She decided she was happier today, even if she did feel lonely sometimes. Those times seemed to be fewer. It's nice to walk down Main Street and be greeted with a smile or a friendly, "Hi, Roz" or "Hi Rose." Did it really matter to her which name they called her? She decided she didn't care which name they used. But somehow Roz sounded more citified. Rose seemed to fit Nuna Lake. It's nice to have someone know your name. It's fun to have lunch with friends and to know that that friend can call you if they have a need. It's fun to be in Sarah's, helping customers and helping Sarah plan for the holiday season. And Mike. Would her friendship with him turn into anything more? She wasn't sure but after thinking about it she decided she still wanted him for a friend. It had been almost eighteen years since his wife died. She could see the pain in his face as he had recalled her death. He was a very young man then. He has found a new way of life and seems very happy and content with it. Can I be content to live out my life alone she wondered? Now that she had started to let other people into her life, she was enjoying things so much more. Could she ever let another man into her life and know that the relationship might not lead to marriage? But if it did lead to marriage was she willing to take a risk that she might end up living the same life style as she had with Rob?

Finally she decided it was too much heavy thinking. She would take one day at a time.

Chapter 6

That night as Mike prepared for bed he was thinking about the changes in his life that he was making since meeting Rose. He liked having a nice meal and someone to talk with about his day. He liked it when she had phoned just to hear his voice. When he first met her, he had felt stirrings in his soul that had been absent for years. Since Jean had died so many years ago he had not allowed any such feelings into his life. Jean was his lover, his soul mate, suddenly snatched away from him when they should have had so many more years together. How could he suddenly be disloyal to her memory? He and Tim had made a good life together. They had each other. He was embarrassed as he thought about the inane line he had handed Rose about a rose garden for Rose. He cringed every time he thought about it. But Rose had looked so sad, so vulnerable, he had felt a need to take care of her and make her smile. But when he started to call her Rose instead of Roz, did he overstep his intent? He was only trying to be kind. Or was he? No one could ever take the place of Jean in his heart but was Rose finding her own place in his life? Tim was constantly talking about Rosie this and Rosie that. Mike knew Tim missed a mother figure in his life. The more he thought about it the more he knew he'd reached a decision. Yes, he knew he, Mike, wanted Rose in his life. Someone to laugh with, to share stories with, to talk about his day. Rose had been hurt badly. Could she ever let someone into her life again? And if she cannot, can he be satisfied with what she can share with him? He finally got to sleep and had a restless night of tossing and turning.

Chapter 7

When Rose went to Sarah's the next day, Sarah was filled with new ideas. She found that the store next to her shop was going to be vacant. She decided she wanted to move into the larger space. She wanted Rose's opinion about whether or not it would be a good idea. It would give her more square footage for merchandise. But she had questions. What type of things should she bring in to sell in the additional space? Did Rose think they could attract enough customers? Rose felt completely out of place trying to talk about the logistics and the business side, but she did know customers. And she knew the quality of merchandise needed to attract the high-end shopper. They talked together getting one good idea after another only to then decide it was no good after all. Sarah had already talked to the bank about the financing she would need in order to make the move and that seemed to be no problem.

"When would you plan to move?" Rose asked.

"I'd like to do it in the next three months so I can get the Christmas traffic. I'd like to have one section that would feature one-of-a-kind items so that each customer would have something very special. It's a risky proposal but I'd like to try it. I'd like to have a small corner set aside so that the shopper could have a cup of some flavored coffee. Not a whole shop, but somewhere to pamper the customer." Sarah was excited about the prospects.

Julia, who was keeping one eye on the store and one ear on the conversation, suggested that they plan a special area for gift-wrapping.

But could they really accomplish so much so soon? Sarah would need to order more merchandise to fill the shelves and she would need more display cases. Sarah decided to call a local builder to give her some context of time and money needed to accomplish this so quickly and call some suppliers. Julia would run the shop. Rose would come up with the plans for presentation.

Rose went home very excited about planning out the new shop. The planning skills she used when she planned big events helped her to get organized. She started to fill sketchpads with ideas. She seemed to lose track of time as the day flew by. When Mike called to say goodnight she was filled with news about the new project.

"Well, maybe you're too busy for my news," he told her. "Do you have time for company next week? GreenMower wants to send a rep out to see the mowers. Apparently they have a new ad campaign coming out and may want to feature them. They seemed very excited."

"This is exciting news," she said. "Of course they can come although why they're coming instead of just asking us to ship the mowers is more than I can figure out."

"Who knows? Maybe they'll want to buy them."

"I can't imagine that. What'll I say to them?"

"Rose, you're an intelligent woman. You'll know what to say."

Rose paused. For a moment she was remembering how Rob had lost his temper once when she'd made a decision without consulting him. How different for someone to tell her that she'd know what to do.

"I don't deserve such a good friend as you are, but what would I do without you?" she asked.

"That's what I need. To be your good *friend,*" Mike said in a mocking sad voice. Then he started to laugh and went on. "There is something else, though. There might be a photographer from *Classic Homes* coming. There's a possibility that they might do a spread in their magazine."

"*Classic Homes*? You're kidding. I know that high-class magazine. Wow, I can't believe it."

Thunderstorms moved into the area during the night. With the noise of the thunder and the flashes of light from the storm, on top of her thoughts that kept moving from lawn mowers to display cases, Rose had a restless night. Even before she heard her friendly "Goooooood Morning, America," Rose was out of bed and in the kitchen. I need to get my thoughts going in a different direction. This is a soup day. She started the preparations. With soup, you need fresh bread. She had dough in the refrigerator so she took some out and shaped two loaves. She thought she would take the bread and some chicken soup to Millie and then invite Mike and Tim for a quick supper. She cut up some fresh fruit for a salad. As she worked she remembered her thoughts of the evening before about Mike and about Tim. Would whatever direction she and Mike decide to go leave a bad impression on Tim? A little voice inside her said; *take one day at a time.*

While the soup was cooking she checked her e-mail and was happy when she saw a letter from Jenny.

Dear Mom,

I wanted to let you know that I am in the outskirts of the Sudan. We had a good flight and the people here were so glad to see us. You would not believe this place. I bet it was beautiful at one time, but all we see now are wall to wall people; people who do need help. There is no transportation here. Some people have walked more than 50 or 60 miles or more to get to this refugee camp. They had no food, no water, and only the clothes on their backs. They walked through rebel fighting where the young girls were almost always captured and raped. Some were killed. I'm told that some of these people owned big estates at one time, but you wouldn't know it now. I don't think anyone weighs more than 50 pounds. But they are so grateful to be here. My first job was to ladle out food. The line never ends and we give them such a little bit of food. We sleep in tents with mosquito netting over us. They sleep lying on the ground among snakes, rocks, and the deadly bugs. Today they asked me to organize some games for the kids. Carrie helped me and we tried our best. Someone found a small ball, so Carrie found a stick and took some of the older kids and had a game of sorts. I started to work with the toddlers in the area, but most had no energy and didn't want to leave their mothers' arms. Don't worry about us. Carrie and I are both doing fine. I'm so glad I am having this experience. I'm getting the hang of the language. I heard from Jeff and Karen about your weekend together. Wish I could have been there, too. They're really impressed with you and all you are doing, Mom. Jeff was really taken with Tim and the canoe. It sounds like Mike is being very good to you. You deserve that, Mom. I love you and will write more later. Jenny

Rose was filled with love and pride as she read the letter over and over. Her Jenny - trying to make the world a better place.

She called Mike and asked him to stop by for soup on his way home from work. She said she'd call Tim and invite him. Tim was very pleased to get his own invitation and asked to bring his best friend with him.

As she made her way to Millie's later that day Rose hoped that Millie might feel like talking more about her life with

Harry. Roz wondered how they got through the rough times that seem to invade every marriage from time to time.

Millie said she would like a bowl of soup as soon as Rose arrived, but said it would be much more enjoyable to have it with Harry. Rose told her there was enough for both times but Millie said maybe she wouldn't be as hungry and it wouldn't taste the same. She and Harry had always enjoyed going out to eat and trying new things.

"We will pretend tonight that we are in a Paris cafe enjoying some homemade American chicken soup."

"Let me set the table for you to make it authentic," Rose suggested, and with Millie telling Rose where to find things, Rose transformed that section of the kitchen into a French cafe. Rose could tell that Millie was pleased to see some of her pretty dishes again when Millie gently ran her hands around the edge of the plates. Rose put candles on the table and even got out a bottle of French wine that Harry had been saving.

"Do you have a special dress that Harry likes? Would it make you feel special to change into it?" Rose asked.

Millie ran her hand over her hair. "Yes, but it's my hair that's bothering me. I haven't been able to get a good shampoo for ages."

"I can help you with that," Rose told her. Rose sat a chair by the bathtub and asked Millie to sit on it and lean her head over the tub while she turned on the shower. "Millie, your hair is beautiful. So soft and white. And look at the natural curl you have."

"It used to be a beautiful brown. You are making me feel young again. All we need is some hair dye."

Rose started to laugh and said, "Don't you dare change the color. You are beautiful." She helped Millie change into Harry's favorite dress.

"Tell me about your wedding," Roz asked.

"We were such children; I was sixteen and he was eighteen. It was wartime. We had just my family there. Our minister came to our house for the service. Then we went to an inn on the outskirts of town and he left the next day for the Pacific. I was still in High School so I went back to school. When Harry came home we moved to Nuna Lake. His family had found us a small apartment so we could have our privacy." Her eyes were filled with the memories she was reliving. "We had three babies within the next five years. My dear mother-in-law was so good to us. Harry's dream had been to go to college and it was a dream his family really wanted for him. I had crammed three years of college into the two years Harry was away so that sweet woman baby-sat with the children while Harry and I both went to school. As soon as I finished my last year, I taught school to support us so Harry could go full time. When he finished, he took over the Hardware Store when his father retired. I stayed home with the children. We have had a very good life."

"How did you know he was the one for you?" Rose asked.

"I guess just the way we felt when we were together," she told Rose.

"Did you ever regret leaving your family?"

"I missed them terribly but I had no regrets. My Harry was wonderful to me about making trips back to see them. And when they came to visit he was so good to them."

"Tell me about your children. Where are they now? Do any of them work with Harry?"

"My Harry's a very wise man. He encouraged them to find what would make them happy and then go for it. Our oldest son is a doctor in Boston. Our daughter is a professor of English Literature on the East Coast, and our youngest works in aerospace. They all want us to move closer to one of them, but Harry and I are happy here. The day may come when we have to move, but not yet."

"Was Harry disappointed that none of them wanted to take over the family business like he did?"

"No. Harry wanted them to be happy. Harry thinks that the day of the family owned hardware stores is coming to an end. All these super big home improvement stores are taking over. But that's OK. Harry will close the doors on his store when he retires."

Knowing that it was about time for Harry to come home, and time for Mike and Tim to come to her house, Rose told her goodbye.

She timed it perfectly. Mike and Tim and Tim's friend, Allan, walked in the door as she finished the preparation. They talked about the graduation ceremony set for the next day and Tim's plans to go to California to attend Stanford University in the fall.

"Why did you choose that school?" Rose asked.

"That's where my mom and dad went to school. My grandparents live close enough to the school that I can go there on weekends to see them."

"That's the best reason I've ever heard," Rose told him. "I know you'll be very successful there."

"Yea, but this will always be home. As soon as I get my degree I'll be coming back here. The old man there can hardly make it to work some days and someone has to keep the family business going. I'm going to fix an old tent for him to live in. Maybe I'll let him visit the big house sometime. Anyhow, enough of that. I need your opinion on something. I have an idea about those old tools of yours, Rosie. I think I should investigate about them before you give them away or try to sell them. Maybe I'll take them to George Markham. I'll show them to him and see what he suggests."

Rose told them about the sketches she was working on for Sarah. Mike asked to see them and declared that they were very, very good. Tim asked about the colors they would use and suggested keeping it *earthy* so that bright plants could be added in various places in the shop. He made an x mark on the sketches where he thought they should go.

"Now that sounds like a salesman or good son," Mike told him. "I gather you are planning to choose our most expensive plants?"

"Yes, if you will give me a commission. Rosie, if it's OK with you I think I'll load up those tools tonight and take them with me."

After the boys had loaded the tools and gone, Mike and Rose sat on the porch swing.

Rose said, "I can't believe where I am today. Last year at this time I was so frightened of the future and today I have so many things going on. I have a beautiful home. I'm enjoying my life. Mike, I really do owe you so much. You have made my house a home with all this beauty. I remember when you told me I had to plant the spring bulbs. I thought no way. You told me I had to plant them so I would feel like they were mine. You were so right. I felt so much pride when I saw them break through the ground in the spring. I felt that both the bulbs and I were putting down roots. And I felt really important when you told me there would be a rose garden for Rose. My first guest here was Judy Martin who came because she wanted to show her mother the flowers. Actually, I think she helped me break down the barriers I was putting up around me."

"Rose, I might get tired of all the people in this town knowing all my business, but there is something special about them knowing when it's time to keep quiet and time to speak up. I guess that's why I stay here. Everyone in town was waiting for the right time to make you a part of our lives. No one knew anything about your past, whether your husband had died or you were divorced or even if you were fighting a serious illness. But they were content to wait. Little by little you started to smile more, walk a little straighter, and well, like I said. These people are special. Now they feel you are so much a part of their lives, it's like you were always here."

Rose asked Mike if he was disappointed about Tim going to school so far away.

"Well, I wasn't sure he would go there. He took a long time settling on a career path. And it may change a dozen times. I know he may not come back here to join the business. I'd be thrilled if he did but don't tell him I said that. I don't want him to feel any pressure. Tim's very much a Nuna Lake kid. We've taken some vacations but he is always anxious to come home. It'll help him, I think, that his grandparents are so close to the school. In spite of the distance, they've worked very hard to stay close to him. His aunt and uncle and cousins are there too, so I think he'll be fine. We'll be going out early to get him settled in before classes start. Did he tell you that he's valedictorian of his graduating class? He has to make a speech tomorrow. He's been practicing like a politician. I know he's happy that you will be going with us."

Mike and Tim came for her the next morning. The ceremony was being held in the stadium. It was a perfect day, sunny but not too hot. The crowd was large. No one seemed surprised to see Rose there with Mike. She had truly become one of the crowd.

Tim came over to see them wearing his cap and gown with the gold stole and gold tassel. His dad gave him a hug, trying to cling to him with one hand and push him away with the other. Rose was glad for both of them and their relationship with each other. Tim's speech was so heartfelt, but funny at times as he reminded his classmates of some of the more interesting times of their lives. Times when maybe they were a bit inquisitive about life.

"You guys had to go home and face your dad and mom," he told them. "I had to go home and face my dad........and 100 moms. Fifty of them would have already called my dad and told him what was going on. The other fifty would have cuffed me behind the ears and threatened to tell my dad."

Laughter filled the stadium from parents who were nodding their heads. He truly was a son of Nuna Lake.

After the ceremony the crowd made their way to the Lake

House where a big buffet had been set up on the lawn for all the grads and their parents. Rose asked if it was appropriate for her to attend and Mike assured her it was and that Tim would be disappointed if she didn't. And it was OK. She felt very much at home there and was surprised by how many of the people with whom she was on a first name basis.

Tim left with his friends. On the ride home, Mike told Rose that the rep from GreenMower would be in town on Tuesday around noon. They would be coming directly to her house.

Rose couldn't figure out why they'd come so far for old lawn mowers but decided to say nothing. Perhaps that is how they do things she thought.

On Tuesday morning she dead-headed some flowers so the gardens would look fresh, and made a pitcher of iced tea and fixed a tray of cookies that she placed on the table on the front porch. The two men arrived promptly at noon.

"Mrs. Graham, thank you so much for letting us see the mowers. We were so surprised to find that anyone had five of them as old as these. And I understand they're in excellent condition. I'm Jim Ward, representing the company, and this is Julian Whitney."

Rose shook hands with them and then showed them the mowers that were still on the porch.

Jim Ward was very excited when he saw the mowers. "The very first mower was built in England in 1830. This is an old Hills Archimedean Lawn Mower. It was probably built around 1890. And here's another, a Henderson. They were usually painted bright red. Here's one of the first power mowers, a Silens Messor, probably built around 1890. This one's a Charles H. Pugh. And this Jacobsen mower was probably built around 1920. One of the first ones they built. This is wonderful."

I wish Mike was here Rose said to herself.

Jim was very pleased that the mowers were in such good condition. "They have obviously been taken care of very well while they were being used. They show signs of storage, but also signs of care."

Rose noticed that Julian was roaming around the yard enjoying the flowers. When he came back to the porch he looked very pleased. The two men talked quietly with each other.

Rose invited them to have a glass of iced tea and they accepted as they sank into the big comfy chairs on the front porch.

"Mrs. Graham," Jim began, "I don't know if Mike Nelson told you about our plans. GreenMower will soon celebrate one hundred years of business. When we heard about your discovery of the mowers we were surprised but pleased. We want to show how lawn care has changed over the years. The use of your mowers would enable us to do so. We are planning a big ad campaign both in gardening and technical magazines. We would like to feature your mowers in our campaign."

Julian then began to talk. "When we heard about the discovery of the mowers by Mike Nelson we had what we think is a very good idea. We know that his gardens are famous all over the United States and Canada. When we heard that he had discovered the lawn mowers in Nuna Lake we began to make inquiries to see if he had done any gardens where the mowers were found. We were so delighted when we found out he had designed your gardens."

Julian paused and then continued. "I represent *Classic Homes*. Mike Nelson's gardens have been featured twice in our magazine which is one of the high-end magazines published in the country. We'd like to feature your home and gardens in an up-coming issue. The story will include information about finding the old lawn mowers, which with your approval will be featured in ads by GreenMower. May we have your permission to take the pictures and use the story?"

Rose wished she could talk this over with Mike. But then she thought - why? I am an intelligent woman. I can make decisions that concern me.

Jim then interrupted, "Do you plan to try to sell the mowers? Mr. Nelson told us he didn't know your intent."

"Mr. Ward, you and Mr. Whitney take me by surprise. I had no idea they might be of interest to anyone. I really wasn't sure what I'd do with them. I'll have to think on that. You certainly can use them in your ads, though. As for the article in your magazine, well, it sounds like it would be something very nice."

"We'll need to bring in a small camera crew to get shots of the gardens." Julian said.

"I don't see any problem with that. But I would want you to get Mike's permission and coordinate the time with him if his name's in the article."

"There's one thing we should discuss," Julian said. "Money. Most people are very happy to be featured in the magazine. We don't pay the owner for the use of the pictures. We would, however, be happy to make a sizable donation to your favorite charity or group."

Rose's first thought was of the shelter. "Is there an amount of contribution you would be considering," she asked.

"That would remain to be decided but I would think in the area of $2,500 or $3,000. But your group would also be mentioned which would give you some good publicity."

"I would like that. Do you have an idea of when you might take the pictures?"

"As soon as possible. I'll get in touch with Mike Nelson and we'll set a date. Then I'll advise you," Julian said. "Do keep in mind we might need two days or more, depending on the weather."

Jim then asked, "One more thing, might I take the mowers with me today? Headquarters is most anxious to see them."

"Of course," Rose told them.

I wish Mike was here Rose thought after they left, and felt greatly relieved when he pulled up in the driveway. She ran out to meet him very excited with her news.

"Rose, sit down and tell me what happened."

While she was telling him she could see that he was obviously pleased that his work would once again be featured. He said he'd make time to help them whatever time they chose. Then he started to laugh. "Did you tell them you were going to toss out the mowers? What are you going to do with them?"

"I was so surprised by their words I didn't know what to say. I was trying to play the cool levelheaded businesswoman who makes decisions all day but I was churning inside," she told him. "I think I'd better give the mowers to them."

"I think that would make them happy. But why not let them make the next move? Who knows, they may make an offer to the Women's Shelter if they don't want to pay you. I'd play it cool for a while."

"When Julian talked about the money all I could think about was the Women's Shelter. Do you know how many cans of paint $2500 would buy?"

Mike gave her a hug as he laughed and said "A lot of paint."

"Mike, I thought maybe you would stop by earlier. Did you stay away on purpose?" she asked.

"Only partly. I've been driving around the area waiting for them to leave. I was so anxious to hear what was being said I almost hid in the bushes. But I knew it was not my business. You're a strong woman, Rose. You don't need anyone telling you how to make decisions. I didn't want to influence whatever decision you might make."

"Would it be silly to call Tim and tell him the good news?"

"He'll be really excited. Because he and the crew did so much of the actual work here I know he'll want to take ownership for it. Call him on his cell phone."

When she gave Tim the news, Rose heard him shout out to the crew around him, "Rosie's gardens are going to be in a magazine. And we did it!" he shouted. She could hear the whoops and calls from the crew. Roz felt like every one of the crew belonged to her.

Mike looked around the porch, now nearly empty except for a couple of boxes. "What's in the boxes?" he asked.

"I couldn't make much sense of it when I looked inside. It's probably nothing important."

Mike opened the top and pulled out some papers. "These look like notes from the gardener. Mind if I take them home to look at tonight?"

"Not at all," she told him. "Unless you find something really interesting will you please just throw them away? This will leave me with a canoe and a desk and then maybe I'll even put my car in the garage."

After Mike left, Rose was bursting with excitement to tell someone about it. What should be first - an e-mail to Jenny, a call to Jeff or her Mom or Sarah? Just then the phone rang.

"Hi, Rose," came the familiar voice of Judy Martin. "Hope I am not interrupting anything."

"Judy, I'm so excited. You'll never guess what's happened. I'm going to have money, a lot of money for our women's shelter project."

"What are you talking about? You know we're going to ask merchants for donations."

"You don't understand, Judy," Roz told her and then proceeded to tell her of the events of the day.

"I'll be on the phone all day telling everyone," Judy said excitedly. "But I almost forgot. I'm calling for a purpose. On the Fourth of July some of us old fogies choose to celebrate a part of the day together. After the parade we go to someone's house for a picnic. This year it's at our house. In the evening we go to the concert. Some will stay on to watch the fireworks and the others will go home. We want you and Mike to be here."

"I know I'd like that and I think Mike would like it too. Tim's going camping with the guys but as far as I know Mike is free. What would you like me to bring: dessert, salad, meat? Think on it and let me know."

After hanging up, Rose checked her watch and decided that even with the time difference it wasn't too late to call her mother.

"Mom, I have exciting news for you," she said cheerfully when her mother answered. "You could never guess all the good things that are happening. My old lawn mowers are going to be featured in ads for a lawn mower company and my gardens will be featured in *Classic Homes*. Even my picture might be there." She then proceeded to tell Ann all the details. "And they will even give a donation to my favorite charity."

She told her mother about her new projects for the women's shelter and also about the expansion of Sarah's shop. When she told of their plans to have one-of-a-kind items, her mother told her that she had come upon such a shop in London. She, Ann, would look into the resources there.

"I need a new project and it sounds like fun to research it," Ann told her. "Rosie, you sound like a new person. I haven't heard you this enthused for many years. I am so happy for you. I know you'll miss Jenny this coming holiday. How do you plan to spend the day? Jenny said it was wonderful last year with so many things to do."

Roz shared her plans for the days ahead. "Mom, I've made so many new friends. They are so friendly and kind. When I'm walking downtown or in a store there's always someone to call me by name."

"Tell me about Mike. Is he part of the reason you're so happy?"

"Yes, Mom, he is. He's very caring and kind to me. But I do think his heart still belongs with his wife who died shortly after Tim was born." She then told Ann the story of Mike's past. "I really feel that Mike and I will always be very, very good friends. But that's as far as I think it'll go."

"Tell me Rosie; are you afraid to let it go further? Are you afraid of being hurt again?"

"Maybe," Rose answered truthfully.

"Well, you don't have to be in any hurry to decide. If it's meant to be, it will be."

"I want to do the right thing, Mom. I don't want to make a mistake and hurt someone else or maybe let myself get hurt again."

"You don't have to be in a hurry. Take each day as it comes. Did you get your appointment set for your mammogram?"

"Mom, I've been so busy I forgot. I'll call tomorrow."

After a little more chatter with her Mom, Rose went to the computer to write to tell Jenny the good news, and then she phoned her son.

Jeff and Karen were really impressed when Rose told them. They were familiar with the magazine. "It's like a dream book of the rich and famous," Karen told her. "I want all my friends to see it. I'll buy all the copies in the store."

Over the next few days, Rose's phone rang non-stop. Everyone in town wanted to know what day the photographers would be there. Rose realized that this was not a Rose Graham event. It was a Nuna Lake event. She felt good to be a part of something that was bringing joy to Nuna Lake.

Chapter 8

Mike felt like he had found a treasure trove in the box of papers he brought home. The gardener had apparently experimented with different ways to fight the diseases and insects that go with gardening. He had none of the chemicals used today, but with roots and herbs the gardener had tried different combinations. Some of them worked; some were not successful. Then he'd try a different combination. He had kept meticulous notes on all his endeavors. He recorded the amount of the item he had used and how often he used it. He experimented with the placement of the plants in different places in the yard. As Mike read the notes, he felt humbled by all the information now available that made his life so much easier. Yet this intelligent gardener had done it with his skills and determination.

There were books and notes from each year. What could Mike do with all these notes? He knew he could never throw them out. Perhaps he should just take care of them for a while. Maybe some student, some day, could use them in writing a thesis. As he started to put things back in the box he found another notebook he had missed.

This book was filled with information on the old Hicks family; the flowers and bushes the mother had loved; the trees that gave the father pleasure; and how he had planted to please the young daughter. One time he planted a garden that spelled out her name, using flowers that began with each letter of her name. On one of the pages was a note about the *udelida adusgi*. Now what in the world is that, Mike wondered? As Mike started to read he thought it must be a flower or tree. Certainly one he had never heard of. As he read on he finally figured out it must be the name of a garden. He read about a creek and a small waterfall and a pond. It appeared it was in the woods on the back part of the property. Mike finally began to figure it out. It was the Cherokee name for secret garden. Apparently this gardener had built it for the young daughter. He wrote how she took her favorite doll to the garden. Later the notes mentioned how she would go there to write in her diary. And even later Mike read how the gardener worried when he saw her take a young man there. His notes showed he worried that it might have been wrong to create this hidden place for her. Mike began to wonder just where this garden was and if he could uncover it. He decided to try. Should he tell Rose about it? Wouldn't it be something if he could restore it and *then* show it to Rose? The more he thought about it, the more he liked that idea. He looked back through the notes for land-mark trees for he knew it was probably grown over. Except..... the creek should be able to lead him to the garden. He decided to search for the site.

During the next couple of weeks Mike was pleased that Rose was spending so much time at Sarah's. He didn't have to explain why he was in the woods by her house so much. And he was glad that he didn't have to report to anyone at work. He spent the biggest part of a day tramping thru the woods. He found a few small streams that went nowhere. The second day he searched in a different area but he found nothing .Maybe it's dried up and I'll never find it, he thought. The next day he was back, tramping in yet another area. He finally found another small creek. As he followed it he went back and forth thru brush and bushes. He kept going. When he saw the land drop sharply for a distance of about four feet he realized that this could be the place. He examined the earth where the water dropped. There was a natural stone wall there. Could there have been a pond at the bottom? He pulled apart some of the weeds and reeds and decided that there had been a pond there at one time. As he explored the brush area he found the remains of what had one time been a stone bench. This had to be the place of the secret garden. As he let his eyes roam the area he tried to imagine how he would make it happen for Rose.

With a goal in mind and a self-imposed deadline looming, Mike began to make the secret garden his top priority. He decided to build up the edges at the top of the waterfall so that the water flow would be a little narrower at the top and rush a little faster and fuller as the water cascaded down. The pond that had been there was totally filled with weeds, reeds, rushes and other growth. The water apparently left the pond through an underground spring. That area would have to be totally cleaned out, he thought. He might put in some water lilies there. Ferns around the edges would look good, too. Perhaps some red-twig dogwood or holly bushes with red berries for color during the winter. There were a lot of dead limbs and many, many, wild grape vines that would need to be cleaned out. How could he get it all done so quickly? Should he ask for help? No, he decided. I want this to be my project. Something I do for Rose. He decided he would think about the plantings as he cleaned up the area.

That night, Tim asked his dad where he was all day. "You didn't even have your cell phone turned on," Tim told him.

"Was it anything important?" Mike asked.

"Oh, no," Tim answered. "You know that place runs by itself. I just wondered what the big deal was."

"Well, Tim, if you must know, I'm considering a new project and I need time to think about it before I talk about it."

Knowing this was often the way of his father; Tim shrugged his shoulders.

Chapter 9

The photographer and his assistant from *Classic Homes* arrived early Wednesday morning. He made notes of the natural lighting and then moved all around the property to get the various views. When a small crowd of Nuna residents stopped by to visit Rose, she asked the photographer if she should send them away. With a smile he told her he often has an audience. As long as they stayed out of his way, they wouldn't bother him. Then he told her he wanted to take some shots of her, perhaps in one of the gardens, or sitting on her porch. She started to protest but then decided, why not. He decided it might provide some human interest if he took pictures of Rose's neighbors enjoying her gardens. The people were thrilled to think their picture might appear in a magazine so they were happy to roam through the yard.

Mike had also been asked to appear in a few pictures. When he arrived the photographer complimented him on the beauty of the gardens. He told Mike how much pleasure he got when he saw so much of nature's beauty.

After pictures had been taken of all the gardens, the woods, etc., the photographers took a break for lunch and then started all over again to get the pictures in a different light. When Mike found out the photographer wanted some pictures after dark Mike invited them all to go for dinner and then come back to the house to get the shots with the landscape lighting.

It was a very exciting day for Nuna Lake and the people kept coming all day. The photographer was able to finish up his work that evening and Rose hoped to get back to normal the next day. She learned the magazine would be issued in about three months but they would send her an advance copy.

Rose settled into a routine. She usually left fairly early in the morning for Sarah's to continue planning for the move next door. They had lots of work to do if the new shop was to open so quickly. The builder Sarah had contacted told them he would do his best to meet the schedule and had started the renovation that same week. Sarah had contacted some suppliers for fixtures and they had agreed to rush the shipment. Rose knew that some of the refinement might need to be made later but they could make the move. The specialty areas could also come later. Sarah and Julia were impressed with the sketches Rose had drawn. It was going to take a tremendous amount of work. There were storerooms to set up with shelves of many sizes. Which new display cases would they buy and/or take from the present shop? What kind of flooring would they use? What about the lighting? How long could the old store remain open while getting ready for the move? Sarah, Julia and Rose were in and out of the new location constantly.

"What does Bob say about your plans for your shop?" Rose asked Sarah one day.

"It might end our relationship," Sarah told Rose. "He is very disappointed I'm making this move. He hoped I would sell the shop and move to Atlanta. He wants me to come to Atlanta, get married and have children. I want to get married and have children too but I just don't think I could ever be happy in Atlanta. I guess we're at a stalemate about what to do."

Customers came and went while they worked. One morning Will Laughlin walked in the store.

"Well, what good luck I'm having today. I just found three beautiful women in one place." In a playful manner he gave each of them a hug and then told Rose he was pleased when he heard how famous she was becoming.

"Whatever do you mean? I'm not famous."

"Then why am I being paid to come and talk with you?" he asked.

"What in the world are you talking about? Quit teasing us."

"Well," he began slowly as if to keep them in suspense longer, "It seems like you had some old lawn mowers that are now going to become famous. And it seems your beautiful gardens will become famous. I got a call asking me to help with the cover story about the history of Nuna Lake. They called me because they knew I was finishing up a book on this area of the country. I told them I supposed I would have to do it," he ended with a droll sigh.

Rose, Sarah and Julia laughed and were excited by the news.

"Wonderful, wonderful." they cried out. "When will you start?"

"Actually, I started last week," he told them. "I have a brief outline written that deals with the town and its background. But I have very little on the Hicks family. I'm here to see George Markham for that part of the article. And I want to talk with Mike about the actual gardens. I thought I'd stop here first to say hello. But what in the world's going on? Are you rearranging the shop completely?"

Sarah was full of enthusiasm as she told him of her plans. Rose, feeling like a business woman, then turned to him to ask him why he came there to shop. He was so well traveled he could have shopped anywhere.

"Nothing looks touristy, or is that even a word," he asked.

"When I come in the shop I feel like I'm important. Merchandise is attractively displayed. The quality is top-notch and you go the extra mile like gift-wrapping. I feel like I'm giving a really special gift. It's hard for me to shop. I hate big cities but sometimes it's hard to find nice things in the smaller towns."

Sarah was beaming when he was done. "I'm certainly glad you found us. And I'm happy that you were the one chosen to write the story to go with the pictures. How long will you be in town?"

"I have a flight out early tomorrow morning so I'm hoping to complete my notes today. I'm headed out to see George right now. I need to call Mike to see if he has time to see me late this afternoon. Do you know if he's in town? I'd like to meet him for dinner if I can get it arranged."

Suddenly Rose had a brainstorm. "Mike is coming for dinner tonight at my house. We're having lasagna. Why don't you join us there? Sarah, why don't you come too. Then after dinner the guys can talk gardening and we can finish up our presentation plans for the one-of-a-kind area. We really need to come up with a name for it. What do you think? Would that be OK?"

Sarah looked a bit surprised but said it was OK. "But I have to leave early. I have an eight o'clock appointment for my mammogram in the morning."

"Which reminds me that I still need to make my appointment," Rose said. "I'm going home and call right now."

Rose had everything prepared when Sarah, Will and Mike arrived. They ate out on the patio. The bright white flowers seemed to glow in the candles that were placed on the patio wall. And the fragrance of the garden was enticing. Mike and Will had made a quick tour of the grounds before they ate so that Will had a feel for the article.

After eating, Mike and Will went into the living room area to talk.

Rose and Sarah sat at the kitchen table with their plans.

They made a few additions to the drawings which Sarah said she'd take to the contractor in the morning. "Did you remember to call for your appointment for your mammogram?"

"Yes," Rose told her. "They want me to get copies of my prior mammograms for comparison. I called the clinic where I used to go and they are sending them to me. See, I did remember," Rose said with a smile.

Mike walked into the area and asked the women to come and join them. "Rose, I think you should hear some of the history of the house."

They joined the men as Will related what George Markham had told him.

A wealthy businessman from New England, a Mr. Hicks, was moving many miles away to Chicago to build a new business there. His new bride was sure that she could not stand the heat of a city after growing up around the ocean breezes so refused to move. He told her he would find a place with cool breezes, close enough to the city, so that she could live there in the summer and he could commute on weekends. Shortly after the move she gave birth to their first and only child. The man looked for property for a summer home - east, west, north and south. One day as he was out traveling, he met someone who told him about a big, beautiful lake, surrounded by big spruce trees. A very tranquil lake, he was told, with hidden fishing ponds. As he was looking at the lake an old Indian man came by and they began to talk. When the Indian found out that Hicks wanted to build a house for his wife and daughter there, he took Hicks to a special place. High above the lake was a plateau. The air was clean and fresh and the view of the lake was magnificent. Hicks decided this is where he would have a home built. He asked the old Indian for help in clearing the site for the house and for a wide pathway up the hill. He had decided to have everything arrive by boat from the other side of the lake so he could preserve the woods. It was quite an undertaking since everything had to be carried up to the site.

Hicks had decided on nothing but the best as the home was being built. Little by little the home was completed. The wife was thrilled with the house and spent every summer there. She delighted in having guests come to stay with them. There were guesthouses built on the property. They spent time in and on the lake. Canoeing was a big sport. There was fishing and croquet and badminton. There was horseback riding along the trails that soon developed. In the evenings the guests would play bridge or play billiards. Many evenings were spent enjoying music or reading poetry. But soon others wanted to build there also. Parts of the property began to be sold. Roads were built and before long stores appeared, then cars and gas stations, etc.

Their daughter eventually grew up, married and had a family. Her family spent many summers at the house. Then it was grandchildren who lived in the house. As Nuna Lake became more of a town, each generation who were descendents of old Mr. Hicks had less and less interest in the house. They felt it was too far away, or needed too much upkeep, and a variety of other concerns. The house had been empty for about 15 years when finally it had been sold about four years earlier. Then that buyer was transferred and the town people were concerned that it would never be restored. They were delighted when Rose bought the house and they saw it come to life again.

Mike then told them of growing up in Nuna Lake and hearing the stories that were handed down. Every one was in awe of the Hicks house and the family. "Everybody in town loved that house when I was quite young. Every blade of grass was manicured. At one time they had a gardener there three days a week. But one summer no one came, nor the next. The local families who had always opened the house for them were told not to bother, that the family would be traveling abroad. The property became neglected and overgrown."

Rose sat and listened to Will and Mike. She suddenly

remembered the old diary that had been hidden in the floorboards.

"Wait right here. Don't anybody move." Rose said as she hurried up the stairs. "I just remembered about a book that was hidden under the floorboards."

As she came back down the stairs she started to tell them about the book – no names, just initials – no dates.

"Then it could date back to the original owners. It was the custom of the times to use initials. Have you read it?"

"Yes. I was feeling sorry for myself one day so I had a good cry while I read it." She told them about the contents.

Finally, Will said he needed to leave as he expected a call from his publisher. "Would you mind letting me borrow the book for a while? I'd really like to read it."

"Of course, you may. You may find the makings of a whole new novel," she told him.

Will laughed and said he could never write a novel, that he was too technical.

Sarah told him she was sure he was wrong but he'd better not start it tonight as she needed to get home.

Will and Mike also said it was time to go, so they said their goodbyes.

As they walked to the car Will asked Mike if he had uncovered anything else that might make the story interesting.

Mike hesitated and then said, "I think you have the story now."

Will looked at Mike and knew there definitely was more to the story. Sometimes, things just need to be kept private.

Chapter 10

Once again it became time for Rose to take a turn at the women's shelter. She and Diane drove together wondering what chore awaited them. They rejoiced over having some funds coming in and probably decided on a dozen things that should take priority.

Fran Farrabee, the manager, was always glad to see them.

"Diane, Rose. I'm glad to see you. I don't know how I'd manage without you. Things are a mess in the kitchen. Grace hasn't been able to come in all week and the kitchen looks terrible. One of our guests had four kids who were hungry all the time. We had a couple of spills out there while they were here. The kitchen really needs help. I'm so glad you're here."

Roz and Diane got busy. Roz started on the refrigerator and Diane started on the food pantry. Next they cleaned the stove, the outside of the dish cabinets and the tops of counters. The kitchen was small and rather dingy but at least now it was clean if someone needed food. As Roz and Diane drove home they talked about their own nice kitchens and how badly new equipment was needed at the shelter.

"I don't think the freezer is working well. There was so much ice in it," Rose told Diane.

"Maybe we should put that on the list," Diane answered. "Do you think there's room for anything else on the list?" she said with a smile.

They talked a few minutes about the trouble that brings people to the shelter. "Sometimes I wonder how I could ever live through anything like that," Diane said.

"I know it's very, very hard for them," Rose answered. "And it's very difficult to make decisions when you're so upset. At least we can help them have a safe place for a while"

"Speaking of safe, Al Barnard thinks we should include a high quality alarm system for the building. I asked him to get some estimates on what it would cost," Diane said. Al was the chief of police in Nuna Lake.

"That's a great idea. Did you know that he's asking people to donate their old cell phones so that the police can give them to the battered women?" Rose asked.

"Isn't it nice that the people of the town are becoming so aware of the whole situation of abuse?" Diane added.

They then decided to lighten the mood so they bragged about their children for the rest of the drive home.

Rose was pleased to see a letter from Jenny on her computer.

My dear Mom, What wonderful exciting news. My beautiful mom has her picture in a magazine. I'll be home when it's issued and I plan to buy my own special copy. Thanks for the box you sent. The balls, the dolls, and the stuffed animals really made a hit. I think it is the first time the kids have ever seen anything like it. After they hold the dolls, they pass them on to other little ones nearby, and so on. They loved the jump ropes. The kids are so sweet as they share their things. I almost called the other night. I really missed you. It had been a very sad day for me. They asked me to work in the medical tent because I can understand the languages a little easier than some people can. A woman who had malaria was brought in on a stretcher. She was trying to hold on to a baby about six weeks old. She handed me the baby and then closed her eyes. The medic could do nothing for her. She died about an hour later. I just sat there holding this little baby, trying to sing to him, or trying to get him to take a little nourishment, but nothing worked. He also died. I cried and cried. One of the aid workers came and took the baby and then told me I had five minutes to dry my tears, that there was another baby there who needed me. It makes me so sad to think about all the money I have wasted that might have saved lives. Somebody has to do something to stop this madness that is going on in the country. Sorry if I am spouting off too much. I guess I just miss you. I'll see you around Labor Day. Don't worry. I'll be OK.   Love, Jenny

Rose sat and cried as she read the latest letter from her daughter. No parent wants their child to see such things, but how much worse it is for the children who are trying to live thru such chaos. She could feel Jenny changing, maturing. But more than that, she had a sense that Jenny would seek a new trail to blaze. She would have a refined set of values. Rose hoped that Jenny would always be able to keep her smile and her ease of comfort with people.

Rose sat in the darkness of her front porch that night saying a prayer for her daughter and all the sons and daughters of the world who are facing such challenges. At times she felt almost embarrassed that she was having so much joy in her life and Jenny was having the opposite types of emotions.

On the morning of the Fourth of July, Mike called Rose and suggested that she go on to the parade with the rest of the crowd and then he would join her at the Martins for the picnic lunch. Rose asked him if everything was OK and he said it was, but Rose had a feeling that he had something on his mind. He did seem to be putting in more time at work these days. Maybe some important project to worry about. She recalled the same day last year. It was the day Mike had showed her the full plans for her yard and especially the rose garden. They were hardly more than acquaintances then. Now he was such an important part of her life. Roz also remembered the joy on Jenny's face as she and her friends had celebrated the holiday together. She thought about Jenny and her new mission. Roz became very homesick for her daughter but she knew in about six more weeks, Jenny would be home.

She decided she would drop off her food at the Martins on her way to the parade. They insisted she join them for the festivities. The parade was loud and noisy but fun as the clowns worked the crowd along the parade route. She was happy to see Mike already at the picnic when they arrived back at the house.

"You must have a very big project on your mind," she told him. "You seem to be working a lot of extra hours."

"Well, it's the time of year to keep things moving," he told her. "You look wonderful. I believe you have something new on."

"As a matter of fact, I do. I decided I was tired of looking like a fuddy-duddy. I'm going to invest in a new wardrobe. This was step one."

"Well, red is a good color for you. With your dark hair and your dark eyes, you look like a model. You are beautiful."

"Enough, enough." she said. "You'll make me blush."

They both then went to help with the food. Hamburgers and hot dogs were being cooked on the grill. Along with ham and fried chicken, about four kinds of beans, about six or more salads and a huge table of desserts, the crowd of people all enjoyed the food. While finishing up the lunch with ice cold watermelon, some people began to drift to places where they could relax for a few minutes. Others went to spend some time on the lake, and others went to check on their teenagers. They would all meet up again at the concert.

As Rose walked around the crowd, she stopped to chat

with this one and that. She could feel eyes watching her. And indeed they were. Mike smiled and Rose felt like all was well with the world. She walked over to him.

"What would you like to do?" Mike asked Rose.

"Is there a quiet little place where we could sit and relax along the water?" she asked.

He did know of such a place right along the lake in one of the hidden alcoves. They walked there together and then sat on the beach.

"This reminds me of the sitting rock at the Lake House," she told him. "It is so quiet and private."

"We haven't had many quiet, private times lately," he told her. Then he took her in his arms and kissed her tenderly. "Do you have any idea of how incredibly beautiful you are?"

She didn't answer him at first and then said thoughtfully. "Mike, you've changed my life in more ways than you know. There's more joy and fun, more encouragement, more interest in life. You treat me with respect but more than that you make me feel like I deserve respect. It's been a long, long time since I felt this way, if I ever did."

"Rose, you give me too much credit. You're an amazing, beautiful intelligent woman. You are kind and considerate on the outside but strong and determined on the inside. Many women would have collapsed after the year you had. Instead, you reached out to help others. And the one you helped the most is me. You've made me come to life again after almost eighteen years of living only to raise my son. You make me see things differently – the beauty in a sunset, lights on the lake, little things around me. I never expected to feel that way again."

They sat quietly holding each other close.

Chapter 11

Mike was making good progress with the *udelida adusgi*. After he cleared the undergrowth he realized that there were two big oak trees spaced just right for a little walkway into the area. He trimmed the trees so that they formed an archway as a natural entry there. The pond area had been cleaned out and, after coming over the rocks, the water was crystal clear. He had thought about various plantings he could do, but as he stood there, seeing nature at its best, he decided to keep it very simple. There were already big bushes that would be blooming at different times. The holly trees and bushes with their red berries and the red-twig dogwood would provide color all winter. I do believe, he thought, that all it needs are some ferns and a few small plants for color. And the water lilies for beauty. After wavering back and forth about whether he should be more elaborate, he decided his first decision was best. He gave a lot of thought about the perfect bench - cement or wood, back or no back against the seat. If it's wood, should it be painted, natural or decorated? Though Mike made these decisions daily for his customers, this was different. This was for Rose. It had to be special. He finally decided on a park bench style made of wood. He would leave it natural but treat it to resist the elements. And across the top of the back, he would paint her name there between two very small red roses. That would be the only decoration.

Satisfied that he had made the right decision he could then think about when to take Rose there for the first time. He and Tim would be leaving for a month's vacation. They planned to drive to California, stopping for some camping and fishing along the way. Tim would be staying to go to school after they both had a visit with Jean's parents. He wanted Rose to see the garden before he made the trip. When he got back to the office he realized he had really made all this happen. Well, that shouldn't surprise him, isn't this what he does to earn his living? He began to have doubts that maybe she would think it childlike and silly. Or that he was stupid to have done it. Or is it me, he wondered? In restoring this garden for Rose, I am saying goodbye to Jean. She will always be a part of my past but Rose is my future. Yes, he thought, I really do love her. Then with a smile, he thought, "I am behaving like a teenager. I know Rose. She will like our *udelida adusgi*."

Chapter 12

Rose was very busy with her work at the shelter and help-ing Sarah. The group of women had decided to solicit the businesses in town to ask for contributions. They were over-whelmed with the response. A local builder said he knew the house well and knew it needed a new roof and a few repairs to the structure. He would take care of the structure and see about getting help on a roof. If nothing else, they would have supplies at cost. Harry Moore, privately telling Rose that he would be closing his store soon, made a contribution of all the paint they would need for inside and outside and recom-mended a local painter who he thought might donate his time to oversee the work. A local appliance store said they would donate a large refrigerator-freezer that had come in with a big scratch that they could not sell at full price anyhow. And once the ball started to roll, other contributions started to come in. Fran Farrabee, the manager, was overwhelmed with the plans. Mike sent out a crew to trim trees and bushes and said he'd send a crew to do some more plantings that would not require upkeep after the painting was done.

Sarah planned to close her shop for a week to make the

move into its new home and reopen on Labor Day weekend. A crew of Katy's high school friends had volunteered to come in and help with the move. Rose's mother had connected them to a resource for their one-of-a-kind section and was sending additional information to them.

The copies of Rose's past mammograms had arrived and her appointment was set for next week. Rose would be glad to get that over with.

Mike and Tim were getting ready for their trip. Rose realized how much she would miss Mike when he was gone. She realized that Tim had become almost a son to her, stopping in many times during the week just to say hello or even to ask her advice about women. Tim and Jeff were becoming good friends. They had so much fun on Jeff's visit putting the canoe in the water.

She was thankful that things were going so well for Jeff and Karen. After much thought, Jeff had decided to stay with the bank at this time. She was glad that Jeff and Jenny as young adults seemed to be getting closer than they had as teenagers. She could sense that Jenny was changing. She seemed to be more serious about her life. She had even mentioned going back to school.

The day before Mike and Tim were to leave, Mike stopped by in the afternoon and after a time asked Rose to take a walk with him. Rose walked slowly, stopping to admire her gardens, which were always changing. As they approached the back of the area near the woods, he suddenly *noticed* what could be a path and why don't they see where it goes. Roz decided to play along with his mood.

"Do you think it will take us to China? Or maybe to a jungle in Africa? Or maybe Shangri-La?"

"Maybe into outer space or the future," he answered her. "Let's go."

Hand in hand they walked the path for quite a distance.

Roz kept stopping to admire this tree or that bush. "This is my first trip into the woods," she told him.

She spotted the trees with the branches making an archway. "Look at that, Mike. It looks just like an archway or a doorway. Let's explore."

She hurried away ahead of him. She stepped under the arch and saw the beauty of the hidden garden. She stopped suddenly as if in shock. Then she looked around and saw the bench with her name. With tears in her eyes she ran to Mike's arms. Sobbing, she tried to say something that would truly express what she was feeling. But the words would not come.

Mike held her close. "Why don't you try out the bench?"

With Rose clinging to him they made their way there. Finally she dried her tears and began to look around. She saw the crystal clearness of the pond with the water lilies floating on top, and the water cascading down over the stones, which were rounded by age to a beauty of their own. She was overcome with emotion as she realized how much time and work this had taken. And he had done it all for her. As she walked around the garden she stopped to touch the soft ferns moving gently in the breeze. She put her hand in the pool to touch the water lilies floating on the top. She stood by the bench, running her fingers over her name. She turned to look back at Mike. He was looking directly at her.

"I love you Rose. I'll always love you."

Rose very calmly looked at him directly and said, "And I love you Mike. I will always love you."

They quickly closed the space between them and held each other. For a few minutes they held each other close without speaking. Then they kissed hungrily and passionately.

"I have wanted to say that since the first day I saw you. I need you by my side to make my life worthwhile."

"And I need you, Mike. You make my life complete. You make me feel safe. You make me feel secure. You make me feel like I could do anything. I think about you all the time.

I've been trying not to think about you so much because I was afraid you wouldn't want a loser like me after the wonderful life you had with Jean."

"You, a loser? Don't ever say that again. I held on to memories of Jean because that was all I had. I never met one person who even came close. But you came into my life with all the good things about Jean plus all the good things about you."

They kissed again and again until they both realized that it was not enough. Clinging together they made their way back to the house and Roz's bedroom. Slowly and passionately they undressed each other and lay on the bed, running their hands over each other bodies and awakening desires that had been suppressed for many years by both of them. Finally as their bodies joined, they both felt the fulfillment of the love they shared. For a few minutes they lay side by side in each other's arms saying nothing.

"How did you ever get an idea for something as wonderful as my own special place," she finally asked him. He told her about the papers he had found that told about the Secret Garden.

"It's called an *udelida adusgi* in Cherokee."

"Now I know why you were so busy the last few weeks. Oh, Mike, how can I ever say thank you. It's absolutely the most thoughtful, the most wonderful, the most beautiful....."

"I love you, Rose. I will love you till the day I die."

"I love you, Mike. I feel like I want to shout it from the mountaintops. I never knew real love could make me feel this way."

They reached for each other again and then finally Mike said he had to leave. "I have a lot of packing to do. I'll be gone for a month. How can I ever live without you?"

"Mike, you'll be back. I feel so secure in your love that time and distance will not change us. I'll be here waiting for you."

After a moment she asked him, "What about Tim? Are you sure Tim is OK with this?"

"Tim will be very happy. He wants you in our lives. But what about your family? Will it be hard to tell them?"

"It will be easy. I'll write them tonight. Mike, thank you for this wonderful surprise. It's our own special space. No matter who knows about it, it will always be our garden, our *udelida adusgi.*"

Rose felt like she could explode with happiness. She could finally admit to herself what she had known more every day; she loved Mike and wanted to be with him forever. On any condition. Even if he could never fully feel that way about her. It was so wonderful to feel so treasured and wanted. Now to know that he felt that way too, well, it was almost more than she could stand.

She wanted to tell Jenny but was subdued. Jenny was seeing horrid things and working so hard. Is it right for Jenny's mother to feel like a sixteen-year-old? What words could she use?

She decided to talk to her mother first, even if it was nearly midnight in London. When John answered, she asked him to stay on the line but to ask her mom to pick up the extension.

"I have some news for you. Mike and I are in love."

"Oh, Rosie, we are so happy for you."

"I need your advice about telling Jenny. She is so important to me I want her to know, but is it wrong for me to be so happy when she is going through so much?" Rose asked.

"It is never wrong to be happy. And I know Jenny will be happy for you. She tried very hard not to show you how worried she was. That's why she spent the holiday with you last year. She nearly cancelled her trip to come to Europe. Even when she got to London, she nearly turned around to come back home. We encouraged her to stay to finish her last year of college here. Rose, we've always known how strong you are. We know you had a lot of rough days. But just like you got stronger, Jenny will get stronger. Knowing you love her enough to tell her about an important part of your life will make her happy, too."

After Rose hung up, she went to the computer. As she started to type she received a phone call from Tim.

"Hey, Rosie. Dad told me he loves you. Rosie, I love you too. I'm really happy for all of us. It makes me feel good to see my dad so happy. Now I know he'll have someone to take care of him while I'm gone. Since this is my last night in town how about the two of us do the sights tonight? Maybe we can let Dad come along. We'll start at MacDonald's or Burger King. Who knows where the night will take us?"

"Let me check my appointment calendar. Yes, I can fit you in tonight. Will it be a formal affair?"

"I already got my tux packed so let's go casual. We'll pick you up around six."

"I love you, Tim," she told him.

"We'll see you later."

Rose went back to the computer.

My dear Jenny, If there was ever a time when I wanted you here beside me it is now. I wish I could share with you in person the happiness I am feeling. For some time now, I knew I was beginning to have strong feelings for Mike. He is so good to me. And he is so protective. I feel safe and content with him in my life. Mike's wife, Jean, died shortly after Tim was born. They had a brief but very happy life together. I could see the pain in his face when he talked of her. I really thought that maybe he would never have anyone else in his life that he could care about that way. But I was wrong. Today, he told me he loves me. And I told him I love him. I am not taking Jean's place in his heart. I have my own place there. I feel strange writing this to you since you have not had a chance to get to know him. But I think you will learn to love him too. He is extremely intelligent, but has a quiet, almost shy, demeanor. He is highly respected. I wondered if

I should dare to write about my happiness when you are facing so much death and destruction. But you are my precious daughter, no matter where you are. You are a part of my life forever and ever.   *Mom*

Rose hit the send button and then sat there thinking about her day. Now she had someone to turn to when she wanted to hear a voice. She had someone to hold her close when she was sad and laugh with her at little things. Life is so good for me, she thought.

She phoned Jeff and Karen. She really didn't think they would be home from work yet but she was anxious for them to know about her happiness. She left them a message saying she would call them back later with some good news.

She went to freshen up for her big date but then remembered she had not shut down the computer. She went to shut it down and saw she had mail waiting.

Dear sweet Mom, I guess the vibes we share were working overtime tonight. I couldn't sleep well so went out to look at the stars. I'll always remember how you taught Jeff and me about the constellations and how we would spend evenings with the telescope. The stars are really bright here. I checked my computer when I came back into the tent and there was the wonderful letter from you. Mom, I'm so happy for you. I'm so glad you shared the news with me. I remember meeting Tim when I was there. He seemed like a good kid. That must be because he had a good father teaching him. I'll be home before very long now. I'll be happy to meet Mike. I know he must be great or you would not care for him. With one exception you have a knack for ferreting out phonies. Love you, Mom.   *Jenny*

Mike, Tim, and Rose went to the local cafe. There was no time for private conversations as they ate their burgers and fries. Friends came by the table to say goodbye to Tim. They all had good-natured advice for him and teased him about whether or not he would be changed when he came home at Christmas time. And whether or not he would meet a girl there and bring her back to Nuna Lake or stay true to any one of the girls in town. Teenagers and adults came by to wish him well. They had chosen a good place to eat. Rose and Mike just kept smiling at each other. When Debbie, Tim's almost girl friend came in, Tim left the table to talk with her.

"How did it go telling Tim?" Rose asked.

"When I got home he told me I was looking smug and wanted to know why. When I told him I had told you I love you his first words were to ask if you love me. And when I said you did he gave me a hug. He was really happy. He told me how much it has meant to him to have you in are lives."

"Does he understand that I will never, ever try to replace his memories of his mother?"

"Rose, he has no real memories of her. Only what we tried to create. He had never known what it was like to have a woman's touch or interest until you came into our lives."

When they got back to Rose's house, Rose hugged Tim and told him goodbye. He said he would wait in the car while Mike walked Rose to the door. "I love you Rosie," he called from the car.

"I'll call you every day," Mike said. "If anything goes wrong, call the office. They know you're a top priority in my life. They don't know about the garden, but my secretary started singing love songs every time I came into the office and told me she thought something very important was going on in my life."

"Did you tell Tim about the garden?"

"No, once he made a remark about the time I'd been spending on some project and asked what I'd been doing. When I told him I wasn't ready to talk about it he backed off. Did you tell your kids yet?"

"About us? Yes! I e-mailed Jenny and had a response back

from her almost immediately. She's very happy for us and she's looking forward to meeting you. So are my folks. Jeff and Karen weren't in, but I'll phone them now. I didn't mention the garden to any of them. I sort of think I want to keep it secret between us, at least for a while. It's such a special place. When we do decide to tell them, I'll have the pleasure of talking about it and showing it off." She paused for a minute. "This has been the most wonderful day of my life. I really do love you, Mike."

He held her close and told her goodnight. He and Tim were leaving at dawn the next day.

She heard the phone as she went in the door. As she expected, it was Jeff and Karen.

"What's up Mom?" Jeff asked.

"Mike told me he loved me and I told Mike I loved him."

"Oh, Mom," Karen interrupted. "We're so very, very happy for you. We've known for a long time that he loved you but we didn't know if you were ready to love back. You deserve only the best. When did all this happen?"

"Just this afternoon. I just felt I wanted my children to know. I e-mailed Jenny and heard back from her almost immediately. She's OK with it. At least I think she is. She wrote a lovely letter."

"Believe it or not, Mom," Jeff said, "I know she's OK with it. I can't tell you how many letters we've had from her over the last year saying she hoped you would meet someone worthy of you."

"Stop. You'll make me cry," said Rose, holding back a sob.

"Well, she'll be here soon and we can all get together. Since you don't get international flights into Nuna Lake why don't you let Karen and me meet her and bring her home? Or do you and Mike want to meet her down here?"

"Mike's taking Tim to Stanford. They're driving out,

camping and fishing along the way, and then have a visit with Tim's grandparents. Then Tim will go to school and Mike will fly home."

"So you'll have some time alone with Jenny before he comes back. OK then. We'll meet her and drive her up. It'll give us a chance to visit."

As she went to bed that night she knew it was a day that she would never forget.

Chapter 13

Feeling like she was floating on air the next morning Rose sat down and made a list of everything she wanted to do before Jenny came home. She wanted to give the house a good cleaning and prepare two guest bedrooms with fresh linens. She wanted to get some food prepared and in the freezer so mealtimes would be easy when Jenny came home.

Earlier she had received a lot of information from her mother about the one-of-a-kind shop in London. That shop sold only merchandise that was made by women in third-world countries. These women made pennies a day selling the items to tourists. When it's shipped to the United States or Great Britain, the store marks it up about 300%. The store is run as a charity and all the proceeds are returned to the women. With this money the women can provide for their families. They ship delicate beaded purses, jewelry, skirts, shirts, tops, wood carvings and many other items. Rose wasn't sure it was the type of merchandise Sarah wanted. Only Sarah knew what she was looking for and only she could make that decision. Rose would take the information to Sarah's while she was doing errands. Rose's mammogram was scheduled for this morning so she'd do that too.

She took the brochures and headed for the shop. Sarah was on the phone when she got there.

"It's Will again. Third time this week," Julia said with a twinkle in her eye.

Sarah hung up the phone and rushed to Rose. "You'll never guess what's happened. Will just got the advance copy of *Classic Homes*. He said the article and pictures are great. He's so excited about it. He's going to try to bring a copy to us tomorrow or the next day. Isn't that exciting?"

Hmmmm, I wonder why Will called Sarah instead of me, Rose thought with a smile on her face. Well, it would be nice if Sarah found someone who would appreciate her not someone who wanted to change her.

Feeling happy Rose left the store and made her way to the Health Clinic with her mammogram records. She finally admitted to herself that she was a bit apprehensive about her visit to Dr. Forton. It's a feeling most women get when they go for the test, she thought, especially when seeing a new doctor. Her friends all thought the doctor was wonderful.

"Hi, Mrs. Graham. I'm Lucy," said the nurse as she entered the office. "Please come this way."

Rose entered the inner office area. It looked like every other mammogram examination room she had ever seen. An area to sit while you wait; a room with lockers to change your clothes. Strip to the waist and put on that flimsy cotton top with the string ties that is supposed to be one-size-fits-all but really fits no one. Lucy chatted as she led Rose through the X-Ray procedure and asked her to wait for the results. Soon she came back and asked Rose to repeat the process. "We just need some clarification," she told Rose. After waiting for another period of time Rose was led to another room for an ultrasound.

"Do I have a problem?" Rose asked. "I had some calcium deposits once before and had to go through this same test."

"Maybe that's what we'll see now," Lucy told her. "Doctor Forton will be able to give you more information. You see him this afternoon, don't you?"

"Yes, I'm scheduled at one o'clock. Will he have the results by then?"

"Absolutely. That's the great part about a clinic. We only have to walk down the hall."

Rose got dressed and left the clinic and walked down the street to the coffee shop to get a cheese sandwich and coffee before returning to the clinic.

"Hello, Rose," Dr. Forton said as he entered the examination room. "Would you prefer I call you Mrs. Graham?"

"Rose is fine," she told him as they shook hands.

"I've been hearing about your beautiful gardens. I think all of Nuna Lake was happy to see them being restored. Did I hear right that Mike is on his way to California with Tim?"

"Yes, he left just this morning for a month." The Nuna Lake unofficial newspaper at work, Rose thought with a smile

"Mike's a fine man and a good friend. But let's talk about you. Tell me, have you seen any doctor in Nuna Lake who has your current medical records?"

"No. I haven't seen a doctor since I left the city. To this point in my life I've been blessed with pretty good health."

"That's very good news. I see your doctor there was Ralph Rogers. We interned together in Chicago. He's a fine man."

The long pause made Rose shiver though the day was warm. "Do I correctly sense a problem, doctor?"

He turned his computer around where the old and new pictures were placed side by side and said "I'm afraid so. We found a lump right here." He pointed to the X-rays. "As you can see, it's not present on the mammogram you had taken two years ago."

"Could it be calcium deposits?" she asked. "I had a biopsy about ten years ago and that's what it was."

"I don't believe so but it could be. We won't take that risk. It's time for another biopsy. I would like you to see Dr. Daniels at the University Hospital in Sprucedale. Or maybe you'd rather go back to the city and see Ralph Rogers for the procedure. I do urge you to make your decision soon. Call me in the morning."

Rose's first thought was that she wanted to talk to Mike. Mike had been through all this with Jean. Should she call him? Then a bit of reason set in. He might want to cut his vacation short and rush home. Maybe it is just calcium deposits. I can do this. She remembered how Mike made her feel she could do anything. Yes, I can do this. Mike will be calling in just a few hours. I know that will make me feel better. Then with a touch of nerves setting in just a bit she wondered if she should wait to get the results of the biopsy before telling him. Maybe all her worry is for nothing. Yes, she'd keep positive and not mention it yet. He needs this time with his son without worrying about her.

The next morning dawned bright and sunny. Rose was determined to be cheerful. She got a very early call from Sarah saying that she and Will were on their way to her house with a copy of *Classic Homes*. Rose could hardly wait. This is like Christmas she thought. Rose had never seen Sarah so flushed with pleasure as she came in the door. Is it the article or is it Will, she wondered? Sarah was usually very businesslike and professional.

But Rose had to admit she, Rose, was also excited about seeing the article. The pictures were spectacular. Six pages of glossy color photos. There were pictures of the various gardens. One was just the rose garden with a close-up of Rose. There was a picture of the people of Nuna Lake walking through the grounds. There was a picture of Mike and Rose together. The architect and the owner the caption read. Rose examined it closely. She had to admit they did look like a couple the way they were turned to each other. What would people think? And then she started to smile as she thought why not? Soon the world would know they were a couple. And it felt good.

Sarah offered to fix them some coffee and Will went to help her as Rose sat on the swing to read the article. It was extremely well written. No *dumped divorced woman* who bought the house. It was the *charming and gracious Rosalind Graham who had moved from the city to the enchanting little town of Nuna Lake.* Mike was identified as the award-winning Landscape Architect and Botanist with a mention made of some of his awards. He had never told her about that. Will had given a brief history of Nuna Lake and old Mr. Hicks and his family.

They decided that even if it was early in California, Mike would probably be up. All three of them got on phones when Rose called Mike on his cell phone and read him the article. Mike congratulated Will on his writing and Will congratulated Mike on his skill and creativity and his awards.

As Sarah and Will left the house, Rose observed how protective Will was as he walked with Sarah to the car. Is this the type of thing the people saw with Mike and me, she wondered? No wonder people never truly seemed to be surprised by anything in the town. Just like the town will soon know about my biopsy.

Maybe she should get a second opinion or do you get a second opinion just to get a biopsy? A biopsy is just a test. Or do they sometimes do some of the work? She thought she had read an article that sometimes it's a little more complicated. She couldn't really remember. Maybe I will call Ralph and ask him. As she thought about it she really didn't want to go back to the city. Nuna Lake was her home now. If it should turn out to be cancer she wanted to be surrounded by friends. She had no real friends left in the city. Still, this was a major step and she wanted to be sure she was making the right one.

She did wish Mike was here to tell her what to do. As she had this thought she could once more hear Mike's voice telling her she was a strong woman capable of making her own decisions. She really had no choice in this one. The biopsy needed to be done.

Rose went inside the house and called Dr. Forton asking him to make arrangements for the biopsy.

Two days later, Rose drove out of town to get to the expressway and in about 20 minutes she arrived in Sprucedale. She had spent some time on the internet and found the hospital was rated very high for treatments of all kinds of cancer. She held tight to the thought even now that it might be calcium deposits. The staff members she met before entering the office of Dr. Davies seemed very kind and caring, yet very professional.

Dr. Davies, a man in his early sixties was tall and stately, with a thick head of white hair, and a smile and a firm handshake. Rose liked him.

"Mrs. Graham, may I call you Rose?"

"Of course," she answered.

"Dr. Forton has a very good eye at reading mammograms. I agree with his opinion that we need to perform a biopsy. The lump is probably cancerous. That's the bad news. But there is good news. It appears to be small. I would like to do the biopsy as soon as possible, probably in a day or two. Do you have any questions for me?

"Is it possible it's only calcium deposits?" Rose asked, still clinging to that hope.

"Possibly, but from the shape of the lump I doubt it. I want you to be fully informed each step we take. Please feel free to ask me or any of my staff about questions you may have."

"How long will the biopsy take?"

"You'll be in and out in less than an hour, I think. If my schedule wasn't so crowded today we'd do it now. But we can still do it this week. After we get that report we will decide what we do next."

Rose sat and listened to him imagining the worst of all possible results. Her immediate thoughts were of death, of losing one or maybe both breasts, months of being sick, losing her hair, or........

Dr. Davies interrupted her thoughts. "I bet you are sitting there imagining the worst of all possible situations. Am I right?"

Rose confessed she was.

"I don't want to mislead you," he began, "cancer is always serious and we treat it that way. But if you have only bad thoughts you are not fully informed. Some breast cancers caught early have a 97% cure rate after five years. Treatments today are vastly different than they used to be. Many can be treated with radiation so you don't need chemo. We have a big support staff here at the hospital. They'll be with you every step of your journey. I recommend you have the biopsy done right away and we'll plan the next steps later. And you certainly have the right to get a second opinion. Any more questions?"

Rose decided to have it done right away before Mike came home. The appointment was set for two days later. She still didn't know if she'd tell Mike on the phone or wait until he got home. As she drove home she thought about her children. And her mother. Should she call them? Should she tell any of her friends?

I am strong, she thought. I can do this alone. She decided to tell no one until she had the report from the biopsy. Two days later she was back at the hospital for the procedure.

"I'm sorry, Rose. The biopsy confirms the lump is cancerous. Let me tell you what we'll do," he said gently. "We'll remove the lump and any suspicious lymph nodes and have them tested immediately. If we have all the bad cells removed we'll close the incision and you'll be on your way home. If not, we'll remove any remaining cells before sending you home.

We'll give you an early morning appointment and you'll go home that night."

Dr. Davies scheduled the procedure for the first of the week and recommended she go back to see Dr. Forton for a physical before then so her medical records would be up to date.

Rose left the office with a heavy heart. Her fears and concerns grew heavier on her mind each mile she drove home. Why did this have to happen to her? She had tried to live a good life. The worries seemed to be growing. What if I'm sick for months on end and no treatment works. What if......
The what ifs began to build in her mind. By the time she got home she was shaking with fear. She fell on her bed with her face in the pillows and began to cry. She re-lived all the days after Rob had walked out on her. She remembered how alone she had felt. She felt that way again. She wondered why if it had to happen to her it was happening now, just when she was happier and more content with her life than she had ever been. When she seemed to hear Mike's voice telling her she was strong she pushed the thoughts out of her mind. I am not strong, she told herself. I am not strong. She heard her phone ring but decided not to answer it. She curled up her body into a ball and wept. She thought about Mike. Well, she just knew that when she'd tell him he'd say, *"So long, it's been nice to know you."* He'd been through this once with Jean. He won't want to go through that again. She heard the phone ring again. Go away, she thought. She wouldn't answer it. She knew friends would be kind and try to be helpful but she couldn't stand to see the pity on their faces or hear it in their voices. Maybe she should return to the city. What should she do?

Rose heard a pounding on her door and heard Sarah's voice call out, "Rose, are you home? Are you OK? Rose, do you hear me? Do you need help?" Sarah's voice got louder and the pounding continued.

Rose reluctantly made her way to the door and unlocked

it. Sarah pushed her way into the house, "Rose, I've been so worried. I tried to call you all afternoon. When I saw your car in the driveway I thought maybe you were sick or had a broken ankle like I did." Then she looked at Rose's tear streaked face and softened her voice. Putting her arms around Rose she led her to the sofa. "What's wrong?"

Sarah sat with Rose while Rose started a new round of crying. Finally, Sarah left Rose, went to the kitchen and brought back a cup of tea. Rose began to gain control of her emotions.

"I'm sorry, Sarah. I guess I'm having a pity party."

"Well, it must be a very big party. Tell me so I can cry too."

Rose quietly told Sarah about the discovery of the lump and the result of the biopsy.

"Rose, I am so, so sorry. I want you to know I'll be by your side every step of the way."

"You can't do that. You're moving your store."

"I'm superwoman. I can do both. You're catching this early and I know you're going to get through this just fine."

"You don't have time to help me."

"Sorry, Rose, it's already decided. Have you told Mike about your lump?"

"I just found out for certain today. Now I don't know what to do. After all he went through with Jean's illness I can't ask him to go through it again with me."

"Would you turn your back on Mike if he told you he had cancer?"

"Of course, not."

"I know that Mike loves you, Rose, and I think you love him, too. I think he'd want to know."

"I know he loves me. He told me so before he left. And I love him. Sarah, I don't know what to do." Rose began to sob quietly.

"You'll figure it out. It's all new to you now. Give yourself some time. When are you having the surgery done?"

"Next Monday."

"Rose, you are one of many women going through this. You are aware aren't you, that one out of eight women gets breast cancer."

"That many? No, I didn't know."

"Are you aware that Julia wears a prosthesis?"

"No," Rose said in a shocked voice. "I would never have guessed."

"She's had it for around twenty years now. She's had no recurrence of cancer. She works with the Cancer Society talking to people. I know she'd be happy to talk with you."

"I would never have guessed. She looks so……….."

"Is "normal" the word you are looking for?" Sarah began to laugh. "In these days of breast implants who can tell whose boobs are real and whose are implants? Can I ask Julia to check on you tomorrow?"

"I think I'd like that."

"Enough talk about cancer. Let's get something to eat. Do we raid your frig or eat out?"

When the phone rang later that evening and she knew it was Mike's call, she put a smile on her face as she answered the phone. She decided to wait to tell Mike about the sad part of her day until she had the surgery.

The next morning Julia arrived carrying a box of donuts. "I think we should be naughty today and eat the whole box," she told Rose. "Do you have some coffee already made?"

"This is really, really nice for you to stop by this morning."

"It's always fun to come to your house, Rose. This cancer is just some business you need to take care of so you can be your old beautiful self again."

"Sarah told me you went through this. Were you scared?"

"Actually, I didn't have much time to be scared. I was particular about having mammograms taken because my family has a history of cancer. One day between the mammograms I discovered the lump. I went to see my regular doctor who could feel the lump and ordered a new mammogram. He sent me to see a surgeon who scheduled me for a biopsy right away. The test showed I had a fast growing malignant tumor so he scheduled me for surgery the next day. I had to go home, tell my husband and kids, and buy the groceries and clean the house and do the laundry, well, just be normal for their sakes and mine. The size of the lump and the spread of the cancer to the lymph nodes would have made it necessary to remove most of my breast. I had a choice. Take a chance on removing as little as possible which could increase the odds that it would come back or just have a mastectomy. With my family history it was a no-brainer. I wanted to be around to see my kids get married and have babies. And I wanted to live long enough to keep my husband from ever finding a new wife."

"How old were you?"

"I was forty. Today I'm sixty. That was twenty years ago."

"And it never came back?"

"Nope."

"The treatment must have been terrible."

"Actually, my test results were so good immediately after the surgery they decided I wouldn't need any treatment at all. No chemo or radiation. I had tons of checkups over the next five years, then they spaced them out longer and longer."

"No medicine or anything?"

"Yea, they put me on a new drug called tamoxifen. They told me I would probably have to take it the rest of my life. But after a few years they told me it was no longer necessary.

"It's good of you to tell me all this. If Sarah hadn't told me I would never have guessed you're a cancer survivor."

"There are more and more of us every year. One of these

days we'll have a cure. Now you tell me about you and what worries you the most."

"I guess the unknown. I don't really know what will happen."

"None of us really know what will happen tomorrow. Just take one day at a time. You have many, many friends who will want to be here for you. Don't be embarrassed or afraid to let them help you. I'm sure you would want to help your friends if they needed you."

"Of course, I would," Rose told her. "But do people really want to tell you if they need help?"

"Did you want to tell anyone?"

"No. I didn't know what to do until Sarah almost knocked down my door. But now I'm so glad she did."

"Have you told Mike?"

"Not yet. You've known him almost forever. What do you think he will say? Will he be able to forget about going through all this with Jean?"

"Jean's circumstances were unique. She was pregnant. Today, she might be saved. I think Mike will appreciate that while we haven't yet found a cure for all breast cancers we are able to cure some and we have so many better treatments. I know Mike will want to be there with you. You'll be through all this before very long. And then," she said with a flourish, "you can be our number one spokesperson to share your story and help someone else."

Julia certainly had a way to make a person feel better, Rose thought after Julia had gone to work.

On Monday the day went pretty much as Rose thought it would. Sarah drove her to the hospital and waited with her throughout the day. Dr. Davies kept Rose informed of every thing he was doing as he completed the procedure. Finally Dr. Davies came to give her the results.

"Even though I told you about everything we were doing as we went along let me give you the official talk. We have performed a lumpectomy on your breast. We removed a small tumor and some surrounding tissue. You may experience some soreness or bruising over the next few days but it will go away. We believe we removed all the cancerous cells. We believe a treatment of radiation is called for to eliminate any hidden cells. We implanted small metal chips in the area so that you can receive radiation treatments after you have healed from this procedure."

"No chemo?"

"At this time I don't believe it will be necessary. We'll keep watch on it though."

"When can I go home?"

"Right now. Just don't lift anything too heavy for a few days."

"When will I start radiation?"

"We'll schedule you an appointment with the radiologist after a couple of weeks. We'll let the incision heal."

As Rose got in Sarah's car, Sarah said she was happy to see Rose smiling again.

"I guess I'm just glad it's over," Rose said. "I had visions of them cutting off my breasts. I'm so glad it's over. I guess everyone in Nuna Lake will know about this very soon."

"Well it's certainly nothing to be secretive about. Friends take care of friends. Did you decide about telling Mike?"

"I'd like to tell him in person but I hope someone else doesn't tell him first."

"That's unlikely since he's in California. Did you tell your mother or your kids?"

"Not yet. I'm afraid they will all want to rush here. I think I can handle this for a little while longer."

"Well, just remember you have a lot of friends to help you. Don't be too proud or stubborn to let them."

After Sarah left Rose realized that while she did feel a little tired and sore, she felt much better just to have it over. Maybe I will call my mother, she thought.

"Hi Mom, how are things in London."

"Rose, I am so glad you called. John had a fall and broke his hip. He had his hip replaced and seems to be doing well but it was a horrible shock to us."

Rose made up her mind not to tell her mother at this time about her biopsy. They chatted about John's treatment, then the kids, and then Mike."

"Are you still so happy, Rose?"

"Yes, Mom. He's still on his trip with Tim but will be home soon."

"And Jenny will be home soon. Rose, I am so happy you are enjoying life again."

After a pause, Ann asked, "Rose, I know you well. There's something else going on. I can tell. What is it?"

Rose decided to change her mind. "Well, I went for my mammogram and unfortunately they found a tiny, little lump. Sarah took me today to have it removed. I'm doing fine."

"Rose, you are trying to spare me. Tell me truthfully what is happening."

Rose told her mother the series of events.

"You need family with you. I'll get someone to stay with John and come right away."

"No, no, no. Things are so different that they used to be. I'm going to be fine. Besides, John needs you."

"What about the kids? What about Mike? Have you told any of them?"

"Mom, I don't want a big fuss made over this. I'll tell the kids when they get here. I'd like to tell them when they are together. As for Mike…well, I decided to wait till he comes home."

"Do you think that's a wise choice?"

"I don't know if it's wise. But it's what I think is best to do. Mom, his first wife died of breast cancer. What if he decides he doesn't want to go through it again? I want to see him in person."

"Mike doesn't sound like the kind of person who would run. I think he'd want to be with you."

"I hope he would."

"Rose, promise me you will tell me each little detail. Don't spare any of your pains or concerns."

As Rose hung up the phone she realized she did feel better after talking with her mother. But what about her kids? Should she call them? In another week Jenny would be home and Jeff and Karen would bring her from the airport. She decided to wait until they were together to tell them about the cancer.

The next week, Jim Ward and Julian Whitney came to see Rose and brought her several copies of the magazine. They told her they were very, very pleased with this project. Then Julian presented her with a check from *Classic Homes* for $3,000 for the Women's Shelter.

"Now, about the mowers," Jim began. "They are very valuable to a very small group of people. For instance, the Henderson is quite valuable. It was made in the middle of the 19th Century in England. There were a limited number of them made. We know that not every museum in the country wants to store or show lawn mowers. I do have an offer for you in the event you would like to dispose of them. Our company realizes that Nuna Lake might like one for their own local museum. We would like to buy the other four. If you will include the Henderson among the ones we buy, I am prepared to offer you $5,000."

Rose could not hide her surprise. But she tried to stay professional.

"Let me call George Markham. He's our local historian."

She knew George had been made a part of the story with his history of the area. Rose phoned him, told him about the article and about the lawn mowers.

George was delighted. "I've been trying for years to get a museum started in the space on the second floor of the library. The lawn mower could be the start to getting established," he told her. "Tim brought me the old tools you found. I think we could really have a museum there." Rose then let George talk with Jim Ward about which mower he would select.

Rose told Jim she would accept his offer. She could hardly wait to tell Mike about it but since he and Tim were visiting with the family, she would wait until evening when he would call. She spent a long time that evening, re-reading the article and looking at the pictures. She could hardly believe the pictures she was looking at were *her* house, *her gardens*. A year and a half earlier she thought her world was coming to an end. Even last week she was afraid she was at death's door with cancer. She still felt a little sore around the incision but it wasn't as bad as she had imagined it would be. She could hardly believe her good fortune.

Chapter 14

At last. The big day has arrived. Jenny would be home today. Oh, how lonesome she had been to see her daughter. Even though it had been (with one exception) a wonderful, exciting year for Rose, she would be so glad to have her family together again. Jeff had already phoned from the airport where he and Karen were waiting. Jenny's plane was on time. Around four o'clock this afternoon they would arrive. Rose had everything ready but she went back over everything again. Judy had stopped by late yesterday to make certain Rose was OK and had been able to get ready for company. Rose didn't know how Judy found out about her surgery but it didn't seem to matter. She was a friend helping a friend. Rose had never been on the receiving end of friendship before and was surprised that it made her feel really good. There were fresh flowers in Jenny's room. Her favorite foods were ready. Also lots of corn and potato chips and salsa and cheese dips that Rose knew Jenny liked. She knew her family would probably be shocked when they learned of her cancer ordeal. She was feeling pretty good these days. But she'd be starting radiation soon. I'll take one step at a time she thought. How could she spend the day without going crazy? That day as she did every day, she found time to take a walk to the *udelida adusgi.*

Rose decided to take a drive. She got in her car and drove first by the shelter. There was a construction crew finishing up some repairs. A new roof was already on the building. She could see a painter finishing up the trim. She felt good to be a part of improving the building. She had worked in the office for an hour last week and was pleased to see the contributions of cash were coming in much better than before. There was still a lot to be done though. She saw an old beat-up VW bus in the driveway and wondered who had arrived. She hoped it was not a serious case.

She drove on and on impulse stopped to see Millie. As always, Millie was delighted to see Rose.

"You have a glow today, Rose. Something special must be happening in your life," Millie told her.

"Oh, Millie, you are so right. This is the day that Jenny is coming home. It's been so long since I've seen her. I'm so restless I just couldn't sit still."

"I imagine that Jenny is just as excited as you are. Just imagine, after all she's been through in the last few months, she'll be able to feel her momma's arms around her. It's good for both of you."

"Millie, I want to share some other good and bad news with you. Something I'm not talking about with everyone but you have become very special to me."

"Dear Rose, you are good for me. You make me feel special, too. What is this good news?"

"Mike and I are....well, Mike and I ...."

Millie interrupted. "You and Mike are in love."

"Millie, I'm so happy about that. But the bad news is that I was just diagnosed with breast cancer. I had a lump removed last week."

Millie made her way to Rose and put her arms around her. "I'm very, very, happy to see two of my favorite people finding joy in each other. I am so, so sorry to hear about the cancer. Are you sure?"

"Yes, I begin radiation treatment in a couple of weeks."

"You will be fine. You have the love of a good man, a good family, and a lot of good friends who will be praying for you. Remember God sends rain into our life sometimes but the rain helps us to grow and be beautiful in the sunshine."

"Millie you always know just what to say."

"Even though I know that some of the days ahead will be hard, hold on tight to all the good ones and try to enjoy each day. Take them one at a time. Make every day special and you will never regret it."

Millie is so wise and caring, Rose thought as she drove away. She has embraced her age and grown older so gracefully. Rose hoped she would do the same.

Rose thought she probably should go home and rest. But she was too antsy. She decided to swing by Sarah's. Sarah would be closing her doors for one week tonight. Then she would reopen next door. Everything was ready for the move that so far was going smoothly. Sarah told Rose she had decided to use the resource from London for merchandise for her special shop. Will had promised to help her find a name for it. "I think that I have been so fortunate that maybe I should give some space in my store to help someone else," she told Rose.

Ever restless, Rose finally drove home. Now Jenny's arrival should be in less than an hour. After a cell phone call, Jenny was only thirty minutes away, then fifteen........ Rose went out on the porch to await them.

When Roz saw the car turn into the driveway, she was at the car by the time it stopped.

"Jenny!"

"Mom!"

They stood there holding each other tight, then stood back to look at one another.

"Jenny, you look beautiful. I love your new haircut." Jenny

had left town as a college girl but returned as a woman. She was slimmer, but her body was tight and firm. Her eyes had a serious depth to them but her smile was as radiant as always.

Jenny looked at her mom. "You look terrific, Mom. You look so good to me. Oh, how I've missed you." She gave her mom another tight hug.

Jeff and Karen helped to unload the luggage and they made their way into the house.

"My own room. What a treat," Jenny said as she saw her own bedroom furniture, her own little knickknacks and pictures. "It seems like it's been a hundred years since I had a room to myself. And mattresses on the bed. And clean sheets. And a view from the window. Green trees, green grass, a lake. Wow, I have really missed home."

Ever the mother, Rose got practical. "Are you hungry? What would you like? Are you tired from the trip? Do you need to take a nap?"

Karen brought a small tray of lemonade, cookies and fruit into the room. Jenny said she was not tired but just felt dirty. "I want a real bath," she said. Karen hurried to the bathroom, laid out some big thick bath towels, perfumed shampoos and lotions and turned on the hot water to fix a luxurious bubble bath for Jenny. Karen and Rose left to prepare dinner. When Jenny came downstairs the family of four sat together over dinner enjoying each other and hearing some of the highlights of the past year.

"Well, Mom," Jenny said. "When do I get to hear more about Mike? Is he good enough for our Mom, Jeff? Karen, you are a good judge of character. Does Mike get your seal of approval?"

Jeff said, "Let me start. No one is ever going to be good enough for my mom, but if I had to make a list of men who might be, his would be the only name I could think of to put on that list."

Karen added. "I think he's very nice. I think he's a very good man. I know he adores your mom."

And Rose added, "He makes me feel like I am somebody. I do love him."

Jenny put her arms around her mother and held her tight. "You are somebody. Somebody special. If Mike's even half as good as everyone makes him out to be, I know he's OK. When will I get to meet him?"

"He will be flying home the end of the week." Rose paused. "There is something else I need to talk about with all of you."

"Mom, you look so serious. Is it anything bad?"

"It's not bad now. A couple of weeks ago I had a biopsy on my breast. It was cancerous. The doctor removed the lump and thinks he got it all. But I need radiation treatments to be sure."

"Why didn't you tell us?" Jeff shouted at his mother. "We should have been there with you."

"Mom, we would most certainly have been here," Karen added.

Jenny got up from the table and walked to her mother and put her arms around her. "Mom, you were so strong and brave to go through that alone. Did you have anyone with you? Tell us about how you discovered it and what happened." Jenny paused and then went on. "Were you afraid to tell us? Were you afraid we'd let you down like we did when we didn't tell you about dad and his girl-toy?"

"It all happened very quickly. I went for a mammogram the day Mike left."

"Does Mike know?" Jeff asked.

"No, I decided to wait until he comes home." Rose went on to explain the series of events and treatments. They had many questions for her including a lecture that they must be informed of every step of her treatment until Rose said she'd talked enough

Rose chased the young people out of the kitchen while she cleared the table. She heard Jeff tell Karen and Jenny that he knew Mike loved his mom but he bet Mike would be furious when he found out that Rose hadn't told him what she was going through. But soon it was so nice to hear them laughing and talking, remembering old friends, and childhood memories. Jeff and Karen would be leaving in the morning so Rose was glad they had a chance to visit.

As darkness fell, they took the telescope out to the back yard to look at the heavens. Rose went out to join them and it made Rose feel good when Jeff and Jenny reminded her of the many times she had set up the telescope and taught them about the stars.

Jeff got up early the next morning as Rose was having her first cup of coffee. The day was bright and sunny and he asked Rose if they could have their coffee while sitting on the swing.

"Mom, I'm sorry I yelled at you last night. I don't think I've been a very good son to you in the past. I didn't mean to show you disrespect when I didn't tell you what I knew about Dad. Sometimes I wanted to knock him down. Then I'd remember that it wasn't anything new. He'd always been a jerk. To me you were always the rock of the family. You were always there for Jenny and me. You had a successful business. You always had a smile on your face. I didn't know what to do. Karen and I talked about it but could never decide what was best. To let you live in ignorance about what was happening or tell you and maybe destroy your world. Maybe you'd hate me forever."

"Jeff, I guess there were no easy answers. I was very hurt when I found out what had happened and I was very embarrassed that everyone knew but me. I imagine my ex-friends had a good laugh over it all."

"But if they did that were they really good friends?"

"No, they were not. But I didn't know that at the time.

There was something very artificial about it all that I didn't recognize until I moved to Nuna Lake. It's taken time, a lot of time, but now I realize that if it hadn't happened the way it did I would probably never left the city. Jeff, I do have a good life here. And with Mike in my life I know the years ahead will be even better."

"Mom, I kind of think you made a mistake not to tell him about the cancer," he said quietly. "He's a good man. He loves you. Maybe you're afraid of losing him. It's not going to happen, Mom." He thought a moment. "Maybe I was afraid of losing *you*. Maybe that's why I didn't want to tell you about Dad."

"I guess maybe I'm like you, Jeff. You didn't want to hurt me with bad news that could change my life and I don't want to hurt Mike. He's so good to me and I need him so much."

Jeff reached out to embrace his mom. "You won't lose Mike."

Karen and Jeff left for home with a promise to be back soon. Last night they had urged Jenny to come and spend a week or more with them so she could visit with former classmates and friends who would be in the area.

"I really love that idea," she had said. "I'll let you know which week after I sleep a bit. All the travel and time differences have my mind in a whirl. I guess I need to sleep for a while first."

She slept really late the next morning and when she did get up she didn't want to do anything but relax and talk to her mother. She and Rose sat on the swing and after a few minutes of gossip about this person and that, and hearing again about the surgery, Jenny began to tell Rose about her work in Africa.

"The people were so kind, so appreciative of everything we tried to do for them. Sometimes it was so little that we did do. I've seen a whole new way of life. Many children, even as young as six, carry water from a community well to their homes that are miles away. They're so little and the buckets are so heavy. But it's their way of life. There's very little electricity in the villages where we were. The hospital has a generator that provides power for about three hours a day. They schedule surgery for then. A couple of nights we held lanterns and flashlights. Once for emergency surgery and one night so the doctor could set a badly broken leg. There are so many cases of malaria. Mom, I just can't find the words to tell you how bad the conditions are there. Even the pictures in the news can't really describe the way the people live." Jenny talked on and on about the dire situation.

But Jenny talked also about the beauty of the country and the way the people in their fragmented community tried to help each other.

"Sometimes I would sit and look at the moon and stars. The sky would be so clear you felt you could see into all the galaxies. It was really something. It made you feel that there is hope there. There has to be."

Rose let Jenny talk all day about her experiences, sometimes stopping her to ask questions. It was clear that her daughter had changed in many ways. When she left the summer before Jenny had been a fun-loving, carefree, optimistic girl. She had returned a woman with her eyes opened to the world. She still expressed hope that she could make a difference, but a bit more realistic this time. Rose didn't press her daughter to talk, but she found it very interesting to hear the tales of the people and the country. And she wasn't surprised when Jenny told her she wanted to go back to Africa.

"What would you do there if you went back?" Rose asked.

"I'm thinking about a few things but I need time to rest up first. I think I needed to get home and have my mom take care of me for a while."

"Well, I'll certainly do that. Don't be in a hurry to make decisions. And do try to have some fun. I'm not real sure how you do that at your age around here. But I'm so glad to have you home."

The next few days were all about the same. Jenny slept late, took long walks, and watched TV. She would read and play the piano but did little else. A couple of times she and her mother went into town for lunch where everyone made a fuss over her. They rented DVD's of the movies of the last year and watched them together.

When they stopped in at Sarah's Jenny offered to come back and help finish setting up the new store. As always, Jenny was a stranger to no one. One afternoon she took the canoe to the lake and explored the shoreline. And each night when Mike phoned he talked with Jenny about how she had spent her day.

"Mike has a really nice voice," Jenny told her mom. "I feel like I'm getting to know him. He hasn't even met me yet but he seems to remember everything I tell him about what I did that day. Seems like he's interested in what I am doing."

Rose was pleased at what Jenny said. Then she had a moment of sadness. Rob, Jenny's dad, had made no effort to get in touch with Jenny even after Jenny had phoned him, at Rose's gentle insistence, and left a message to let him know she was home.

One evening Jenny asked her mother about Mike and their romance. Rose was honest with her daughter, telling her about how she had stayed hidden in her home for almost a year, and then finding so many friends. Through it all, Mike had been there. Jenny laughed when Rose told her about inviting Mike and Mrs. Mike to dinner. She was thrilled with the article in *Classic Homes* and proud of her mom for the deal she made on the lawnmowers. She even asked if she could visit the women's shelter.

"Mom, I hope Dad never physically abused you. But after seeing so much this last year, both touring Europe and in Africa, I know that Dad was very emotionally abusive to you. I thought it was so sad when you and Dad split but now when I see you so vibrant, so alive, I am so proud of you for finding a new life."

"Jenny, as I think back on what happened I do realize my part in the whole thing. I knew early on in our marriage that your father had no respect for me or any women. He would flirt outrageously at a dinner party and come home and tell me what dogs the women were. I was never able to please him with anything I did. Instead of acknowledging that this was not an acceptable way of life, I accepted it and turned my attention to you and Jeff. You both were such a joy to me that I let you fill up my life and I could ignore what was happening with your father. I used you both to fill the void that was missing in my marriage. It was terribly wrong for me to do this. I realize now that I set a terrible example for you. Everyone has the right to respect. I was so afraid if I made demands your father would leave me and I would never be able to make it on my own. Well, he left me anyway. It forced me into a new life. I found I could make a life on my own. Now I have Mike and a wonderful new life. I can't imagine why I waited so long."

"You know something, Mom? Every young woman should hear what you just said. You hid things well from Jeff and me. But eventually we did see what was happening. We just didn't know what to do about it. We never felt we had much of a dad and we didn't want to lose you."

Rose was very, very excited the afternoon Mike was due home. At times she was subdued when she thought of the news she would tell him. She decided not to dwell on that now. Even though she had been very happy to have private time with Jenny, she really was very lonely for Mike. She drove to the local airport to meet him. They rushed to each other when he got off the plane.

"I'll never make a trip without you again," he told her. "But where's Jenny?"

"She's waiting for you at the house."

When they pulled in the driveway Jenny came out of the house, held out her hand and said, "I'm Jenny," and then gave him a hug.

"I've never, ever had such a wonderful welcome home," Mike told them.

They sat on the porch that beautiful afternoon enjoying the colorful touches of the beginning of the fall season and Jenny and Mike getting acquainted. Rose thought it was a perfect afternoon with both Mike and Jenny there. Well, almost perfect. A brief shadow fell across her face as she thought of the ordeal that lay ahead of her. Mike offered to take them out to dinner but Jenny told them she was cooking that night and left to put the food on the table. After the dishes were in the dishwasher, Jenny informed them that Sarah was coming by to get her. Sarah, Julia, Katy and Jenny planned to unpack some new cartons of merchandise that had arrived and get things polished for the grand opening.

"We're going to work late so I'm spending the night at Sarah's. I'll see you both tomorrow," Jenny said as she left with her backpack to get in Sarah's car.

"You have a very tactful daughter," Mike told Rose. "And she's almost as beautiful as her mom. Rose, I really, really missed you. Tim and I had a nice time, but through it all we both kept missing you. I never want to take another trip without you by my side. Life's too short to not spend it together."

"I missed you, too, Mike. More ways than you know….." Rose paused. It was so hard to find the words to tell him about the cancer.

Mike began to tell her about the fishing trip and his talks with Tim. Rose sat quietly by his side and listened. Finally, he said, "I'm doing all the talking. It's your turn."

Rose swallowed hard and said, "There is something I need to tell you….."

Mike looked closely at Rose and saw a pained look on her pale face. "Rose, you haven't changed your mind about loving me, have you? Have you met someone else? Are you planning to leave Nuna Lake? Are you….."

"Never, never, never," Rose said reaching out to take his hands in hers. "This isn't easy for me. But I have to tell you. I went for a mammogram the day you left for California. I hadn't mentioned it because I thought it was just a routine check-up. The X-rays showed a lump. I thought it was probably a calcium deposit since I had that happen before." Rose could feel his hands stiffen and become tense. "The results were not routine."

"Rose," he said in a loud tense voice. "Why didn't you tell me right away? I needed to be here for you. Were you afraid I'd walk out the door like Rob did? What was the diagnosis?" His voice grew louder. "What's going on? Do you need surgery? Why didn't you tell me? Did you not feel you could trust me to be here for you?" Rose had never seen or heard Mike become angry. He was frowning and his face was red. His voice became loud and shrill.

"Mike, I felt very confident as I went for the biopsy. Even when they found a lump I was sure it was calcium deposits. I decided to wait for the biopsy."

"Why, Rose? Why wait to tell me? How bad is it?" His voice was a little softer.

"I still kept telling myself the biopsy would show it was calcium. But it was cancer. When Dr. Davies did the biopsy he confirmed the results. He scheduled surgery right away. He said it was a very small lump. He feels confident at this time that he got it all but I will need radiation treatments." Rose paused, pulled away from Mike and sat with her head down and her hands lying limp in her lap. "It was all done so quickly. I wanted to tell you. But I didn't want to interrupt your time with Tim. He'll be changed when he comes home from school. This might be the last time the two of you have such a special vacation."

"Vacations rank very far below your life, Rose. I needed to be with you. You should have told me."

Rose sat quietly for a couple of minutes gathering her thoughts and her courage. "Mike, you are a good and honorable man. I knew you would come home if I asked you. But I also knew it could not possibly be easy for you to go through another cancer illness like you did with Jean. You should not have to re-live it all again. Especially since I was weak and crying all the time. You deserve better. I thought of you constantly and I kept hearing your voice in my mind, telling me I was independent, that I was strong. You make me feel like I can do anything. But, I'll admit I was worried that you would feel you couldn't go through another session of cancer. I won't blame you if you do feel that way. I don't want you to feel obligated to stay with me out of a sense of responsibility."

"Rose, what have I ever done that would make you think that?" His voice was shaking.

Rose had no answer so they sat quietly together, each buried in his and her own thoughts.

Finally, Rose thought, maybe they each needed a few minutes to think alone.

"I'm going to make a pot of coffee," she told Mike and made her way to the kitchen. As she looked out the window she could see him sitting on the swing. His head was bowed with his face buried in his hands. She sat at the kitchen table and did likewise.

After a few minutes Rose looked out the window and watched Mike. The evening dusk was falling but Rose could still see his face. The rage and anger seemed to be leaving but he was pale. As she watched him he placed his elbows on his knees and leaned forward into his hands. She wanted to go to comfort him and be comforted by him. But he seemed deep in thought. Rose returned to the kitchen table and sat there. After another few minutes she looked out again. It was getting dark. She could see the outline of his body. This time he was sitting up straight on the swing but with softness to his body posture. The light from the lamp in the window cast a small glow on the area. He seemed to sense her watching him and looked up and saw her. He smiled at her and made his way to the door. He took her in his arms, holding her tight.

"Rose, I'm so sorry. I'm so sorry you have cancer. And I am sorry that I wasn't here for you when you found out. And I'm especially sorry I acted like such a jerk when you told me. I know you are strong and independent and that's why I love you. But I found out tonight that I'm not strong. I need you Rose. I'll always need you. Please forgive me."

"Oh Mike, of course I forgive you. Will you forgive me for not telling you right away? I should have known better. Down deep I know I did know better." She began to sob. "I don't think I have really stopped crying since I found out. But I *will* stop. I've been very scared. With you beside me I know I can fight this."

"Are you too tired to talk about things tonight?"

"No, but are you? You've had a long trip away from home, a long day today with the time changes and jet lag. We can talk tomorrow."

"I'll sleep all day tomorrow. I want you to know what I was thinking about while I sat on the swing. But first tell me everything about your health. Who you saw? What they said? Tell me everything."

Rose told him step by step what had happened. As she told him of the despair she had felt he wrapped both his arms around her.

"I'm so sorry I wasn't here for you. But I'm here now and we'll go through the rest of this together."

After Rose had finished talking she turned to him and said, "Now it's your turn."

"Rose, I'm going to be as honest as I can. This news did take me back to the early days of my marriage to Jean when we got the dreaded news she had cancer. I was young and didn't really understand that it could be fatal for her. I told everyone I understood, but I really didn't at least not at first. And when I finally did understand I got worried, angry, and upset. I was absolutely sure the doctor had made a mistake. I tried to learn as much as I could about cancer but it was hard to get up-to-date information from outdated journals. Jean was six months pregnant with Tim. Part of me wanted to run away from it all. But out of a sense of love (that I admit felt like a sense of duty those first days) I began to research material pertaining to new procedures that were being tested to try to save her life and the life of the baby. At first I didn't realize that treatment in those days usually meant saving Jean or the baby. But Jean knew and refused to sacrifice our baby. We tried treatment after treatment with no positive results. I remember watching her grow weaker. She tried to be strong through the last months of her pregnancy and looked so beautiful when she held Tim in her arms. But the last six months of her life were spent mostly in bed. I'm not sure how good a husband I was in those days. I was trying to start my business. I know that sometimes I used that as an excuse not to come home. My own mother and Jean's mother took care of Jean, the baby, and the house. Did I really try hard enough? It's true. I could not have saved her life. But I probably could have been a better husband. There weren't too many cancer treatments for pregnant women in those days. But after I sat here tonight, thinking about those hard days, I began to remember how Madonna-like Jean had looked as she sat up in bed holding the baby. How she insisted on soft music in the home and how she read aloud some of the classics which she said would help Tim appreciate the arts. I remembered how I had held her hand as she lay dying. That was when I realized how much I did love her and how much I knew I would miss her. I have let those memories become my way of life for eighteen years. Just trying to live in the past."

"When I met you, Rose, I finally let my heart open up again. I hadn't thought it could ever happen. The first day I met you when we talked about the overgrown trees on your property I felt…..well, something. It didn't feel like another job I would make a bid on to secure business. After talking with you I knew you were going to make this house a home and not just restore an estate. When I found out you had no husband moving in with you I began to take on a responsibility for you. I tried to be sure everything would be done right. I will always have a picture in my mind of the day you planted the spring bulbs. You looked so beautiful that day. You had on a blue shirt. Your eyes were sparkling. When you found out how easy it was you gave me the most beautiful smile. Little things like that made me begin to enjoy life again. When you invited me for dinner the first time I was floating on air. When we began to spend time together I was no longer the fifth wheel when our friends and neighbors met. You let me share my hopes and worries about the kind of man Tim would become. When I saw the joy on your face as you walked through the various gardens it made me feel special. As for the *udelida adusgi,* it was truly a labor of love. I will never forget the look on your face as you discovered it or the joy I felt at being able to do it for you."

He sat silently for a few minutes. Rose sat there quietly absorbing this outpouring of love.

"You know, Rose, you had every right to think I might have stayed out of a sense of responsibility. I was pouting like a child because you didn't tell me something. What would I have done if I had been telling you I was diagnosed with cancer? I don't know how I would have found the words. You deserve better than that kind of nonsense. Rose, I love you and I need you. We'll face the days together but let me be there with you."

"Mike, I love you so much. I know I said I wouldn't cry any more but I can't help it."

Chapter 15

Mike spent the first few days on the computer. He was amazed at how much progress had been made in the treatment of cancer in the past eighteen years. He read each article until he felt he fully understood it. He went with Rose when she met with Dr. Davies and when she met with the radiation oncologist to set up her treatments. He kept urging her to lie down and he would cover her with a blanket.

Jenny took on the role of caregiver. After Mike got Rose comfortable Jenny kept her hydrated with juices and water and fixed her a special diet that she found on the internet. What Mike didn't do for Rose Jenny did. She did the shopping, the cooking and pampered Rose every chance she got. Finally, Rose called a meeting.

"I love all this attention but it's got to stop. The doctor says I'm perfectly capable of a normal life. If I get tired, I'll lay down. If I get hungry, I'll get myself something to eat. And if I have to push you both out of the house so you can have a normal life, I'll do it."

Both Jenny and Mike started to laugh. "I think my mom is getting well," Jenny told Mike.

Mike started to insist on going with her the first day she had radiation even though both she and the doctor told him it was OK for Rose to drive there alone. Then he changed his mind and instead of insisting asked her if it was OK for him to go with her. She smiled and said she'd like that for her first visit. For the next week they settled into a new routine. Mike spent time at work catching up after a month away. Six days a week Rose drove over to Sprucedale for her radiation. Some days after Rose had her treatment, she stopped in at Sarah's to try to help Sarah who was busy after the grand opening. Each night Mike, Rose, and Jenny had dinner together.

The opening of Sarah's had been a big success. The space she had allocated for her special one-of-a-kind items had been filled with specialty Christmas items. Even though it was only September the items were so unique the customers wanted them, some even placed orders for them. Sarah had placed two small tea tables and chairs in an alcove that was defined by the placement of plants where a man could sit while his wife browsed. The appearance she had achieved was that of a sophisticated shop, but once you were inside, it felt homey and small-town cozy. Sarah had hired four of Katy's friends to help customers and keep the shelves stocked. Sarah was already planning how she would decorate and celebrate the Christmas season.

"I can't believe we did all this so quickly," she told Rose. "But I had help from so many people. You, especially," she said giving Rose a hug. "You really made me believe I could do it. The success is beyond anything I expected."

"Rose, have you noticed that Jenny seems rather quiet these days?" Mike asked Rose one evening.

"I have noticed that. I think I'll talk with her," Rose answered.

"Jenny, you seem pretty deep in thought these days. Anything special on your mind?"

"Oh, I'm just thinking about life," she said, "and what I'm going to do with mine."

"Anything you want to talk about?"

"Not yet. When do you finish up your radiation?"

"About another month, I think. Six days a week for six weeks. Jenny, are you worried about me? About leaving me alone?"

"I want to be here for you, Mom."

"And I want you here for as long as you want to stay. But you absolutely cannot put your life on hold for me. I am physically stronger each day. You have a long life ahead of you. I want you to be happy. I sense that you are trying to make career choices. I'm not alone here any more, Jenny. I have Mike. I promise you I will not keep secrets from you again. I'll keep you informed every step of the way. But you must, must feel free to make your own choices for your life."

"Are you really sure, Mom? You're more important to me than a career."

"Jenny, I'm sure."

On Saturday, Jenny announced that if she could borrow Rose's car she would like to drive to the city. She would stay with Jeff and Karen. She wanted to get together with Carrie for lunch the following week and thought she might see some of her old friends. Mike offered his car to Rose. He could always get a truck from work, he told her.

After Jenny left, Rose and Mike took a walk in the woods to their special place. As they sat there relaxing, Mike suddenly got up, took a step into the woods and retrieved a wad of paper.

"How do you suppose this paper got all the way out here?" he wondered. Rose took it from him and opened up the paper.

Half-puzzled Rose said, "This is Jenny's writing." At the top of the sheet were two words. *Why* and *Why Not.*

Mike started to laugh. "She's caught us, Rose. I bet she can even guess what can go on out here."

"But she never said a word. She talked about the beauty of the woods but never mentioned the garden."

"I suspect she found it on one of her walks. The day she brought back the wild flower bouquet I recognized some of the flowers that I had seen near here. I think she realized that since you didn't tell her about it, she figured it was a private place. Let's don't let her know that we know she found it. It looks like she came here to think about her life and make some decisions. This garden is big enough for three of us. But only two at a time," he said pulling Rose close to him.

On Wednesday, Jenny arrived back home.

"That was a short visit. I expected you to be gone for a week," Rose told her daughter.

"Well, I accomplished what I wanted to do. Mike's coming for dinner, isn't he? I'll tell you both then." Rose noticed that Jenny seemed to be like the old Jenny for the first time since arriving home from Africa.

"Mom, Mike," she began that evening, "I'm trying to make some decisions about what I want to do with the rest of my life. Last week I spent a lot of time walking in the woods. I made a list of why I should and why I should not do what I am thinking about. I know you'll support me no matter what I decide. I'm sure you'll do that. I think I know what I want to do but from a practical standpoint I know every job will have its downside. Help me think about them so I won't be surprised."

Rose was puzzled about what she might hear. Ever practical, Mike said, "Sounds like you've given this idea some very serious thought."

"I was really distressed about the poverty and diseases I saw in the Sudan. I know there's plenty of the same in the States. I want to do something about it. I thought about a lot of different ways I could try. I know languages come easy for me and I thought about going to work at the UN. I thought about joining one of the aid groups that are helping in various places in the world. In Africa, I found I do like working with people. I think I've reached a decision. This is why I really need your help. I think I want to go to medical school. The doctors I worked with told me I had good skills with people. In Africa the people skills are almost as important as the medical skills because you have to get the people to trust you. But I want to be able to do more than just talk with people. I want to find ways to stop diseases. I want to work in the medical field. Either working with the people or research."

She went on, "While I was in the city I saw my advisor from school. He reviewed my science class courses and suggested a couple I should take. He will be my advisor in planning my studies all the way. I talked to Jeff and he told me it's possible to get student loans. Then I went to the school clinic and found that I can get a job there to fit around my classes. My work in the clinics in Africa helped me qualify for working there. Now it's your turn. Tell me why I shouldn't try this."

Rose and Mike both were quiet as they tried to absorb all this. Rose finally said, "Well, it will take some years to become a doctor. You'll have little time for yourself. The classes will be difficult." Then Rose added, "These reasons are so superficial. If you think that's what you want to do, do it. What if you do change your mind? People do that all the time. Jenny. I'm so very, very proud of you."

Mike added, "I'm proud of you too, Jenny. You're so talented in so many ways. You have an easy way with people. You're bright and intelligent. That's so important. Go for it."

"When do you think you'll enroll?" Rose asked her daughter.

"Well, actually, since I really couldn't think of any reason why I shouldn't, I enrolled yesterday. I did ask them not to process the papers until I call them, which I'll do the first thing tomorrow. But classes won't begin until January. They did ask me to start at the clinic on the first of the month but I want more time with you. The pay won't be great but the experience and the contacts I make will be good. Jeff and Karen invited me to stay with them. But I think I'll stay with Carrie. She's starting grad school. She has a small apartment close to the clinic. Then I want to move into university housing so I'll be closer to school."

"Jenny, it sounds to me like you need to make this move right away," Mike said. "Are you worried about leaving your mother?"

"I left my mother last year when I should have stayed to help her. I won't do it again."

"Don't say that, Jenny. You worked hard for a year to earn the qualifications for that trip. It was absolutely the best thing for you. Don't ever have any regrets about that. It was good for me to have the time alone. I found that I could take care of myself. I might have depended on you to provide a life for me. I probably would have tried to stay in the city and miss the wonderful life in Nuna Lake. I might never have met or fallen in love with Mike. I have a good life. I want you to have a good life, too. But you have to be ready for it. Go and get your training. But don't ever forget that this is your home. The people in Nuna Lake love you. Don't forget to come back often. I am so proud of you, Jenny."

"Well, you do have Mike," she said pensively.

"I promise you, Jenny, that I won't leave her side. If I think I can't do the job, I'll call you so you can come back to console your mother and yell at me."

Jenny reached out to them both and said, "I need a group hug."

The arrival of the new issue of *Classic Homes* on the newsstand was a cause for great celebration in Nuna Lake. Stores had requested extra copies and even they sold out quickly. The citizens were so proud to have their town presented in such a nice way.

The first call Rose received was from the city - Pat Wilson, the wife of Rob's attorney.

"Roz, dear. I was shocked when I opened my copy of Classic *Homes.* There you were, big as life. Your place looks really classy. How much of the property do you own?"

"Hello, Pat, it's nice of you to call. All the property is mine. I thought the magazine did quite a nice job on the six pages." Rose said with just a touch of smugness in her voice.

"You own all that property? The whole thing? And you hired a famous architect to design it for you? Well, you must really be doing all right."

"Pat, I have never been happier in my life. I have a wonderful life. The scenery is so beautiful here and the people are really special. I have a good life."

"I'd really love to drive up and see it sometime if that's OK. You know, dear, all of us from the old crowd have really missed you. That Rob was such a scoundrel, charming but naughty. I suppose you're terribly busy?"

Rose could just imagine Pat talking with the phone in one hand, the other hand waving in the air as she tried to make a point. Rose had seen Pat's routine many times when she was trying to get an invitation to something she thought would help her climb the social ladder. There were no social ladders in Nuna Lake.

"I live a quiet life up here but I keep very busy. Jenny is back from Africa. She'll go back to school in January to get ready to enter Med School," she told Pat, hoping to change the subject.

"Really," Pat said. "Jenny was in Africa? Well, I must say it seems you are really moving up in the world."

The line went quiet for a moment. Then Pat said, "I suppose you already heard the big news."

"What big news is that, Pat?"

"Tom and I are divorced."

Rose tried to keep her voice calm as she said, "Oh. Well I'm sorry to hear that, Pat."

"Well he was such a jerk about the brooch. I know he's had plenty of affairs. It goes with the territory these days."

Enough, thought Rose. "Pat, dear. I do believe I hear someone at my door. We must talk again soon." And with that, Rose hung up the phone. Then she started to laugh. For most of her life while she was married to Rob, he had held Pat up as an example of the good, dutiful wife. What phonies they all are, she thought.

That night as she told Mike and Jenny about the call, Jenny stopped her mother, got up and told Mike he needed the whole effect. She imitated Pat down to a T, gesturing with her hands and her face.

Rose did enjoy hearing from some of her other friends and colleagues from her working days. They told her how much they missed her and wished her well in her new life.

When Tim called, both Rose and Mike got on the phone. The magazine had also arrived at Stanford.

"Man, I showed everybody the pictures. I told them I helped to plant those gardens. They didn't believe me at first until they saw your name, Dad. I had decided I didn't want any favors from anyone here so I hadn't told them who I was. I only have one class in the school of architecture, anyhow. But would you believe, one day my prof told me he only knew of one other person who sketched their work like I do. His name was Nelson. Since my name is also Nelson, was I any relation to *the* Mike Nelson? He's a big fan of your work, Dad. But he told me not to expect any favors. I've got to earn my grade." Rose and Mike were pleased that he was getting along so well.

Jenny began to get things together for her move to the city. She and Rose shopped for some new clothes, mostly jeans and T-shirts, and a new jacket and other essentials. Jenny had given a talk to the Women's Group at one of the churches about her visit to Africa. When Rose and Jenny stopped at the cafe for lunch, many of the people who knew Jenny came by to wish her well.

"Mom, now I know why you like Nuna Lake. Everyone is friendly. I think I like having people know my name."

Jeff and Karen arrived late Friday night. On Saturday the three young people took the canoe out for one last outing of the year. The trees had all turned to the reds, russets, orange and yellow of the fall season. The water was calm and reflection of the trees was very bright in the water. They were all in a great mood when they returned home and excited about the new cove they had found.

Rose was starting to fix dinner for them when she heard a knock at the door.

Jenny said, "I'll get it, Mom," opened the door and then said, "Dad. What are you doing in Nuna Lake?"

"Well, Jenny, you didn't come to see me when you came home and Jeff never comes to see me, so I had to come up here to see you." He reached to give her a hug but she stepped back from the door. Jeff and Karen told him hello without moving from their chairs.

"Well, Dad, I called you so many times and never found you home. And you didn't call me back, even once. Not even at Christmas. I just figured you didn't want me in your life."

"Of course, I do, Jenny. I guess I didn't get your messages. Barbi's really stupid about remembering messages."

"Hello, Rob," Rose said as she entered from the kitchen. "I'd like you to meet Mike Nelson. Mike, this is Rob."

As Mike and Rob shook hands Rob said, "So this is the famous Mike Nelson. And this is the famous house I read about. Looks good. Looks good," he said looking around. "Barbi was really impressed with the article in that magazine. She'd like gardens just like these. How about it? Think you could fix us up with a fancy lawn like this. I'll pay you double what she paid you."

"Sorry, Rob, I can't do it," Mike told him.

"Think of how much publicity you'd get. I'll have your picture in every paper in Washington. I've got quite a bit of pull there."

"No, Rob, the answer is no," Mike said emphatically.

"I know what you want," Rob said as he rubbed his thumb with two fingers back and forth in a manner indicating more money.

As Mike was telling him, "Absolutely not," Jeff approached his father.

"Dad, I think you'd better leave. Right now."

"Get away from me, boy," Rob told Jeff. "You all think you're so high and mighty up here in a fancy house with a fancy yard. Barbi wants a yard designed by you," he yelled pointing at Mike. "And I always give Barbi what she wants!"

"Well apparently not this time, Rob," Mike told him.

"Rob," Rose began to say, but Rob cut her off.

"Don't kid yourself, Roz," he said with a sneer. "You never did thank me for giving you so much money when I left. I think we should renegotiate the terms of the divorce. I should not have given you a cent. Look how you're dressed. You look like a slob. You never did have any style. I gave you everything. You were......."

"Rob, stop! Right now," Rose said in a clear, strong, firm voice no one had ever heard her use before. "I will not let you insult me ever again. You cannot insult Mike, and you must never, never, be so unkind to our children. Together, we created two beautiful, intelligent human beings. I will try to respect you for that. But that's all," Rose said forcefully. "I was so broken up and sad because of your sneaking ways. You made a laughing stock of me among the people I thought were our friends. I didn't ask for anything from you. I wasn't thinking clearly. But *you gave* me *nothing.* You need to remember one thing. I paid for our first house with the money I inherited from both my grandparents. Your parents and mine paid for most of our furniture. We made such a big profit when we sold the house we were able to buy the second house. So actually, the house was already mine and I should have received half of your assets. Maybe we should renegotiate the terms of the divorce so I get my fair share. I think it is time for you to go. *Now*!"

Rob threw his hands in the air, looked at Mike and said, "See. Now even you can see how stupid she is. No wonder I wanted a real woman."

Mike, with a look of fury on his face that Rose had never seen before, started for Rob, but calmly Rose stopped him. "Mike, he isn't worth your time."

Rose surprised herself that she felt so calm, so in control.

Jeff took his father's arm and said, "I'll help you to your car." Rob pulled away from Jeff and said, "Stay away from me. I'll go on my own. You're as stupid as the rest of them."

Looking stunned, Jeff turned to Mike. "He didn't want to see Jenny or me. He wanted to hire you so he could brag about having the best. I have his genes. Does this mean I'll be that kind of father? How can a father say that to his child?"

Mike put his arms around Jeff and said, "Jeff, you might have his genes, but you also have the genes of your mother. One side will win out, the strong one. And that is your mother's genes."

Rose looked around the room at her family as the door closed. She loved each of them so much. Mike looked angry, Karen looked puzzled, but the faces of Jeff and Jenny were pained and hurting. Jenny began to sob.

"He is so mean," she said.

"The words your father and I said just now should never have been said in front of you. I am sorry. In spite of the way he is today, he was very happy and proud of you when you were born. Try to remember that. I was crushed and embarrassed when your dad left me. But if he hadn't left, I'd still be living that same kind of life, always trying to please him while he lived the life he wanted. I know today how lucky I am. I have two precious children who have grown to be caring, responsible adults. I have the love of a truly good man. I have a beautiful home. I have more beautiful friends than I can name. I've been so blest."

Jeff and Jenny had been clinging together as their mother talked. Karen walked to them and put her arms around them both.

Mike reached out for Rose and held her close. "You are quite a woman."

Then Rose left Mike's arms and gently eased her children onto the sofa. She sat with an arm around each one. Mike and Karen quietly and unnoticed went into the kitchen. For almost an hour Rose and her children talked.

"Did Dad ever really want us?" Jeff asked.

Rose pondered the question for a minute. Then she answered him honestly. "Yes, Jeff, he did. He had big dreams about his son following in his footsteps. He had big plans for you, Jenny. His daughter would be famous. I guess he's completely forgotten all that now. He began to be obsessed with trying to move in the political circles. And more money was always important to him."

As Rose talked with her children, even though they were grown, she realized the power of parents to hurt or help their children. She had a fleeting picture of the children she had stayed with at the Women's Shelter. They were so young. They probably had a lifetime ahead of being hurt unless their mother stayed very strong.

After about an hour had passed, Mike and Karen walked into the room, and sensing that the conversation was a bit lighter and easier than it had been, made an announcement.

"TaDa." Karen said, pretending she was holding a horn. "We have an announcement. We are hungry and this is what we're going to do. We are all going to go into town to the Pizza Palace, eat pizza until we are stuffed and then dance it off. Grab your jackets because it's time to go."

The timing was perfect. They all got into one car and made their way into town. As they were walking through the parking lot, Tyler Lewis, Nuna Lake's traffic cop, was leaving the shop with a large pizza box.

"Good to see you here at Nuna Lake's finest eatery," he told them. "Hey, a strange thing happened here. A few minutes ago I gave a ticket to a guy with the same last name as yours," he told Rose. "He had an address in Washington D.C. I guess he thought he was very important. He was driving like a maniac through town. I sure slowed him down. Is he a relative of yours?"

Jeff answered, "Just someone who has the same last name."

The Pizza Palace was loud and noisy and fun. It was just what they needed. After stuffing themselves and laughing at the antics around them, they all joined the crowd on the dance floor. It was not serious or romantic dancing. It was stomping, line dancing, people dancing every possible style to very loud fast music. Banging on the tin pizza plates. Everyone was laughing, having fun. Every young man there wanted to dance with Jenny and Karen.

As they finally drove home, no mention was made of the events of the afternoon.

They decided to sleep late the next day. When Rose did make her way downstairs she saw that Jenny's door was open and her jacket was gone. The cars were still in the driveway so she knew Jenny must be nearby. By the time the coffee was made, Jenny came in the back door.

"I know this is the last morning I'll be here for a while so I went out for a last morning walk in the woods. It's so beautiful and restful there. I saw lots of little critters: rabbits, chipmunks, and squirrels, and many different birds than I saw before. I saw a blue jay and some cardinals. I love this place, Mom, I really do."

Jeff had made his way into the kitchen and said he needed

food. "Would you make me some blueberry pancakes, oh beautiful Mother-of-Mine?"

"Jeff, you are absolutely gagging me with that talk," Jenny told him. "I want French Toast."

Just then Mike walked in the kitchen door. "Let's let Mike decide," they both said together. Mike said he wanted one of Jeff's super omelets.

Everyone pitched in to cook and soon they were sitting down to a feast.

By early afternoon, Jeff, Karen, and Jenny were on their way back to the city. Rose turned to Mike, seeking the comfort of his arms.

"The last twenty-four hours have been such a roller coaster. I don't know how I'd have gotten through it without you," she told Mike.

"Just like you did with me," he told her. "Rose, you're an incredibly strong, smart woman. It's probably a good thing that you stopped me from hitting Rob. He doesn't look like he works out much. Anyhow, I would have had an unfair advantage; I did some boxing for exercise while I was in college. In your own calm, quiet way you handled the situation. Did you really buy the first house?"

"Yes," she answered quietly. "I was an only grandchild. Both my mother and father's parents had left me money. It was so long ago and I was hurting so badly that I didn't remember it. And I guess my mother didn't remember it either or else felt it wasn't worth fighting over."

"Rose, you amaze me."

"You always know just what to say to me. Let's take a walk."

"Let's rest a while first. You must be exhausted." Mike gently pushed her onto the sofa and covered her with a blanket.

Later that afternoon as they walked out to their own special *udelida adusgi,* they did talk more about the events of the prior day, but that led to talk about their children, all four of them, Jeff, Karen, Jenny and Tim. "We're so lucky to have such a bright, smart family."

Walking toward their garden, Rose told Mike that she thought Jenny had already made a trip to the garden that morning. "She had a calm, peaceful look on her face as if all was right with the world."

As they sat quietly on the bench, the little critters Jenny had seen came to the pond to get a drink. The area looked different now. While the leaves on the trees were just past the point of being bright with color, the dark green of the spruce trees still made a beautiful contrast. One stiff wind would bring the leaves to the ground. Many of the flowering bushes that had surrounded the bench were now filled with bright red apple-like seedpods that would provide food for the wildlife. Only a few chrysanthemums were still blooming.

"Rose, our kids have kept us busy this fall. Getting Tim off to school was hectic. But he's settled there now. Jenny's not only home from Africa, but she's already decided what she wants to do with her life. Even if she later changes her mind about medicine, she's made mature, thoughtful decisions as she plans her future. Jeff and Karen seem very happy. Jeff told me his job is going very well and he may be getting a promotion. I think it's time for us to talk about our future."

"Rose, I love you and I want you by my side forever. If you say we can only be friends who love each other, I'll learn to live with that. But what I really want is to be married to you. Rose, will you marry me?"

"Yes, yes, yes," said Rose. "I want to be married to you."

"Rose, I was so afraid you might not be ready to say yes. But I was praying you would."

"Mike, I love you. I want to wake up in the morning and go to bed at night by your side. I want to share your life, your joys and your sorrows. And even your big beautiful son," she said as she looked into his eyes. "I already feel like he belongs to me."

"And I feel your kids belong to me," he said "Especially, after what happened yesterday. I wanted so badly to be able to take away the pain they were feeling."

"This garden makes me feel magical," Rose said. "I feel like I'm in a dream world floating on a cloud of happiness."

"Can we get married tomorrow or is there a waiting period?" Mike asked with a smile.

"I'm not very experienced at planning weddings. I have no idea. But let's don't wait too long. Life can be so short sometimes. I want to share every minute with you."

The trees shed their leaves as nature got ready for the winter season. The house seemed strangely quiet. No Tim running in and out the door. No Jenny roaming the house and woods. Even though Rose missed them, she knew she couldn't fully describe the way she felt. Happy, elated, ecstatic, - well, no words could express the contentment she felt, knowing she and Mike would soon be married. She knew they had the blessing of their three kids. Tim had given a whoop and said not to get married till he came home. Jenny told them both how nice it was to see them both so happy. Jeff and Karen said they wanted to be side by side with both of them. Jeff said, "Now we truly will be a family, a real family." Her mom asked Rose if they'd set a date, and when she found out they had not yet done so, she said she and John wanted to come for the wedding.

Rose and Mike tried to make wedding plans but always seemed to be diverted away from the actual planning. They were very happy just to have each other. Mike tried to talk to Rose about an engagement ring but Rose was reluctant to talk about it.

"Mike, in my past life I was surrounded by women who wanted and kept getting larger and larger diamond rings. It almost spoiled the beauty of what the ring meant. I have you. I don't need any diamond ring to remind me of my love for you. All I really want is a plain gold band to keep on my hand forever. You're worth more than diamonds," she told him.

Rose and Mike were never exactly sure how the official word got out about their engagement. The ways of the unofficial newspaper in Nuna Lake remained a mystery. But the town did learn the news and calls came from everywhere congratulating them.

Sarah and Will stopped by after work one night with wishes for their happiness. The women she worked with at the shelter planned a celebration lunch for Rose. At work, Mike's staff serenaded him with love songs. They had calls from Don and Beth Cunningham.

Millie Moore phoned. "Rose, I am so very, very happy for you. If you can be even half as happy as my Harry and I have been, I know you will have a good life."

When Rose thought about the actual ceremony, she felt she wanted it quiet and private with just the two of them there. Mike said that was OK with him. They could get married in Nuna Lake, or even fly to Tahiti and be married there. Then they thought about taking the whole family on a cruise and get married on shipboard. They thought about all their friends and decided they should be at the wedding. As they talked about various ideas, they knew they must have their children with them.

"This is the official beginning of making us one family. We all need to be there," they decided.

They thought again about their friends. Some of Mike's best friends were the people he had worked with for so many years: friends who had stood by him when Jean had died, friends who helped to make life easier for Tim. And they couldn't forget about Tim's grandparents. They were like Mike's own parents and they were so happy Mike had someone with whom he could share his life. Mike had business and professional friends from all over the area.

And Rose's friends: certainly Sarah, Julia, and even Katy

from the shop. The women she worked with at the shelter all needed to be included. Her good friend, Lois, from the library. George Markham had even called to congratulate them. When Rose walked on the street in town, strangers stopped her to express their good wishes.

As they talked about it, Rose said, "If summer were coming I would invite the whole town and get married in the rose garden."

"I don't want to wait until summer to marry you," Mike said.

Rose replied, "And I don't want to wait to marry you. Let's think about it later and find something else to do now."

"Sounds good to me," he said, taking her in his arms.

Rose got a call from Judy Martin. "Can you meet for lunch today with our group? We have some exciting news." Rose said she would be there.

They did have exciting news. The shelter was now being designated as a shelter for the whole county. The county would be providing additional funds to add to the money raised by the Nuna Lake women. Adding to the good news was another announcement that was being made that day. A group of women in Sprucedale also wanted to give something to the shelter. They decided to start a program that would aid those women who sought shelter in a long-term way. They would help with medical needs, and would try to help the single parent in this bad situation find housing, a job, and/or day care. It was an ambitious program, but one the group would willingly take on. They asked the Nuna Lake women to please continue the help they were providing so the Sprucedale women could concentrate on their part of the program.

Diane rose from her chair and said she wanted to make a toast.

"Rose, thanks to you, women in this county have a better place to go to when they are in trouble; one that will help them immediately and now, even long term. When you arranged the donation from GreenMower it started a movement in town that everyone wanted to get in on. And now it has spread to Sprucedale and the rest of the county." Lifting up her coffee cup, she said "A cheer for Rose."

"Cheers! Cheers! To Rose!" they said raising their cups.

Rose felt like crying. Could anyone get a nicer tribute? Finally she said, "It's my turn to make a speech. I want to say thanks to each one of you. When I came to this town I was escaping from the city. I didn't want any friends so I tried to ignore you. When you tried to be friendly with me, I turned away. But you people were so pleasant to me in spite of the way I acted. You never seemed insulted or angry when I refused your invitations. And little by little I started to get my life back. I want to thank all of you for your patience with me, and for being such very good friends. When I had surgery you sent food and cards and let me know I was not alone. Sometimes I think my life is so good now I will explode." Rose sat back down.

"You better not explode or Mike will kill us," Clair said. "But let's get down to the really important things. Tell us about your wedding plans. Can we do anything to help?"

"Yes, yes," they said. "Tell us everything."

"Well, there isn't much to tell at this point. I think it'll be a small private ceremony with just my parents and our kids. After all, we are not sixteen any more."

"If you could have any wedding you want, what would that be," Judy asked.

"Well, if we were willing to wait until next summer I would get married in the rose garden. I would invite everyone to share our happiness. But, truthfully, we don't want to wait till then to get married. I think we'll get married before very long and then have a big bash next summer and invite the whole town."

"I think we should get married when Tim comes home

at Christmas time," Mike announced while they were having dinner that night.

"I think you're right. Why don't we go ahead and plan a small ceremony in the chapel and then take the family out to the Lake House for dinner. Then, next summer we can have a big party."

Mike thought this was a wonderful idea and got a calendar. "Christmas is Wednesday this year. If we got married on Saturday we could have a couple nights away and still be back for Christmas morning. Or do you want to plan a long honeymoon? We can go anywhere you like. We could fly to Hawaii for a couple of weeks."

"You know, Mike, we are going to have the rest of our lives to take trips. I like your idea of the Saturday before Christmas. That's December 21st. The church will already be decorated and I can carry red roses. Oh, my, what will I wear?"

"Wear a bright red dress," he answered. "You look gorgeous in red."

"I don't think so," she said.

"Then don't wear anything."

"I'll go nude if you will," she answered.

"Wow. What an idea, a chance to show off my flab. Oops, I meant abs."

Laughing at all the silliness they decided to call the family about setting the date.

"There is something I need to ask you, Rose," Mike began. "Would it make you uncomfortable if we ask Martha and Bill to the wedding? I know they'll love you. They have been wonderful grandparents to Tim and so supporting to me over the years."

"Of course we'll invite them. I'm anxious to meet them. They'll always be Tim's family and that means they're our family, too. Shall I call and invite them or shall we do it together?"

"Mike, where do you think we should live after we are married? I just now thought of it."

"Do you really want to move from this house?"

"I want to be with you, Mike. The house won't matter."

"Then why don't I move in here? You have plenty of bedrooms so we can have all the family here at one time. I don't want to sell my home, at least not now, but I was thinking of a plan. The last time I talked to John, he said he and your mother may be moving back to the states. If they should, and if they don't especially want to live in the city, they could move into my house until they decide where they do want to live," he told her.

"Mike, you are the sweetest, nicest, kindest...." He stopped her words with a kiss.

Chapter 16

There seemed to be a million things to do. Rose wanted to make things as comfortable as possible for the family. Tim's last class was on December 19th. He and his grandparents would arrive in town late on the 20th. They would be staying at Mike's house thru the holidays. Ann and John would also arrive in the city on the 20th. Jeff, Karen and Jenny would meet them and drive them to Nuna Lake. They would stay with Rose. The crowd would all be staying until the first of the year. Rose worked over lists with a calendar in her hand.

Rose decided that both houses should be decorated for Christmas. And of course, both houses had to be cleaned and there was something else, too. A wedding.

Rose felt very satisfied that the plans were underway. She decided to go to Sarah's. She hadn't had a lot of time lately to be there. Rose felt she wanted to explain to Sarah why she would not be invited to the wedding. Sarah had become Rose's very best friend.

Things were going very well in the new location. Sarah had a lot of traffic in the store and sales were good. When Rose arrived Sarah and Julia were going over plans for a very special day on the Saturday before Christmas.

"Sit right here so I can show you my plans for a magical day at *Sarah's Card and Gift Shop*. When customers arrive they will first hear music and a bell. I've invited the Salvation Army to set up a kettle in front of the store. They offered to have their band come and play Christmas carols for the first hour. There will be a red carpet on the sidewalk to draw the guests in. We'll move our coffee cart close to the door so that they can be offered hot coffee or hot cider. High School choir members will take care of that and also do gift wrapping that will be free. I'm trying to find a baby grand piano that I can put in a corner for soft music in the background. I'll hire a musician to come and play Christmas music."

"Does this sound too ambitious or silly?" she asked Rose.

"I think it sounds wonderful."

"Oh yes, there is one more thing. Now don't laugh. Promise me you won't laugh. Will wants to rent a doorman's suit with a big hat and open the doors for people."

"I think it sounds just wonderful. It will certainly be something the people in Nuna Lake haven't seen before." Rose looked around the shop. "This place looks great. I would never have thought that you could pull it off this quickly. I just realized how much I've missed being here lately."

"We missed you too but you'll be back soon. Thanks to you we made the move. You always had so many good ideas and you were so encouraging to me no matter what I wanted to try. How can I ever thank you?"

"Well, you might start by telling me about this *Will* thing. Seems like I hear his name mentioned a lot these days. What about Bill Johnson?"

"Bill and I decided that we probably would never be happy in each other's world so thought it best to call it quits. Will is just great. He's very busy on the road, but he does manage to get here almost every week. He really seems interested in retailing. He asks so many questions and has such good ideas. His eyes see everything no matter where he is. He brings me suggestions that he sees other places. But we're just friends."

Julia, who had been listening as she worked on the books, looked up over the reading glasses perched on the end of her nose, gave a very fake cough and said, "Yeah?" Then she turned to Sarah and said very innocently, "Oh, I'm so sorry. Did I interrupt?"

Laughing at Julia, Rose gave Sarah a hug. "I'm so happy for you." Then she went on. "I did come today with a purpose. I have news for you. Mike and I set the date for our wedding. It will be on the Saturday evening before Christmas. You both have been more than good friends to me; you both are like my sisters. I do hope you'll understand when I tell you I won't be inviting either of you to the wedding. We're going to be married in the Chapel with just my kids and my folks and Tim and his grandparents there. Then we're going to the Lake House for dinner. I'd like to have had the whole town to help us celebrate our day and have it in the rose garden. We can't do it at this time of year. We don't want to wait till summer to get married. So we made these plans. I hope you aren't hurt. I don't want to offend you or lose your friendship."

"No problem," Sarah told her. "We'll still be best friends."

"We're happy for you and Mike," Julia continued. "Anyhow, we'll be busy at the shop all day. At least I hope we will."

"I know you will."

Rose decided to stop by the local dress shop to see what might be on the rack for a wedding dress. She didn't want anything too fancy but something special. When she went in, Janie Carter, the owner, already knew about the wedding date and offered her congratulations.

"I'm very flattered that you came here to shop. I don't

know what type of dress you are looking for or whether I have something suitable in stock. But I think I can help you."

After looking at the dresses Rose knew Janie was right. Nothing jumped out at her as *the* dress. Janie asked Rose to have a seat at a table and then brought out four big books of dresses and bridal gowns. "Look through these books. If you see something you like, mark it. I'll be happy to bring in six or more dresses for you to try. Are you a size six?" she asked.

"More like a size eight, I think."

"Well, I'll have both sizes sent to me. I'll probably be able to have them here by Monday of next week or Wednesday at the latest."

Rose finally chose four. One was off-white chiffon with full, long sleeves, a V-neck with a tight fitting bodice and a full skirt. One was an A-line sheath in delicate pink with a brocade jacket. There was a two-piece silk dinner suit in winter white, with a few glass beads that were supposed to pick up the light. The last was a pale blue dress with a high neck, fitted long sleeves and an ankle length skirt. Rose asked if the dress she chose would have to be ordered. Janie told her the dress she tried on would be hers.

Feeling good, Rose called Jenny and then Karen and asked each of them to stand by her side when she and Mike exchanged vows. After they agreed she asked them to go shop for a new dress that she would buy for each of them.

"Tell me," Rose began, "have you seen any dresses lately that you like?"

"No, no," each of them said. "That's not the way it's done. You pick your dress first and then we coordinate with you. Have you chosen a dress yet?"

Rose talked about the four dresses that were being shipped to Nuna Lake.

Karen said, "I know what we'll do. Call us when the dresses come in and we'll come up and go with you when you try them on."

Mike and Rose called her parents to tell them the date. With all four of them on the phone extensions they felt like they were in a room talking about the plans.

"John, I hope you and Ann will be able to come for the wedding. I know it's important to Rose to have you here. If it's important to Rose it's important to me, too. I know you're giving some thought to moving back to the states. I'm planning to move here with Rose. My house will be empty as soon as Tim goes back to school. Please know you are welcome to move into my house any time you want for as long as you like. It will give you time to decide where you want to move permanently."

"Mike, that's a very generous offer," John said. It's much too generous an offer but it sounds wonderful. Let me talk it over with Ann."

A few days later they phoned back to say that if Mike was still sure it was OK, they would make their plans to move into the house after Tim and Martha and Bill went back to California.

"This is very, very generous of you, Mike," John told him.

"John, I would do anything in the world to make Rose happy. And I know that having you and her mother here will make her very happy."

One night as she and Mike were having dinner, she suddenly thought about their wedding dinner. "Mike, did you make reservations for the family at the Lake House?" she asked.

"I didn't even think about it," he answered.

"I'd better call them right now."

When Dorothy Haskins answered the phone at the Lake House, she offered her congratulations. Rose explained about their wedding plans and said she would like to make reservations for ten people after the ceremony.

"Oh, my," Dorothy said. "We're closed to the public that night. There's going to be a private party here. Christmas, you know. But I hate to disappoint you. We do have a small private dining room that I think is big enough. It's somewhat soundproofed. We'd be very pleased to have you come here if you think the room would be satisfactory."

Rose checked with Mike and they agreed it would be fine. "One more thing off the list," she said.

Janie called Rose early the next week to tell her the dresses were in. Rose called the girls who said they would make a one-day trip up and back that same week to see them. When they got to the shop, Janie had set aside a large dressing room for them to use and had chosen some accessories to go with each dress so they could get the full effect. She even had a bouquet of artificial flowers for Rose to hold while she looked in the mirror.

The dresses were all beautiful. Rose tried on the longer pale blue dress. Then she tried the pink brocade and the white chiffon. But when Rose tried on the winter white dinner suit they all knew that this was it. It fit Rose perfectly. The beading was exquisite. Not flashy at all but elegant.

Then they began to look for dresses for the girls: Jenny, with her dark hair and dark eyes and Karen, the blue-eyed blond. Suddenly, Rose cried out, "I've got it." I want you both to wear winter white."

"I don't think so," they both said. But Rose insisted. "We'll all carry red roses. It will be beautiful."

Janie agreed with Rose. The suits the girls chose were not alike but both were beautiful. Rose could see that each girl was pleased. Janie suggested that Rose have a white ribbon on her bouquet and the girls have red ribbons.

On the morning of December 20th, Rose awoke to her usual wake-up call from the radio. She lay back under the covers thinking about how her life had changed. She felt closer to her children than she had ever felt before. She sensed that they both were at a good place in their lives. Jeff and Karen were both young professionals, doing work they liked to do.

They had a beautiful home, they had good health and they had each other. They seemed very close, but not in a demanding unhealthy way. In a way that says *I'm here for you.*

Jenny loved working in the clinic which made her more anxious to start classes in January toward her goal. The year overseas had matured her. She would get serious much more quickly, but still focused on her goal to change the world. She seemed to be most happy when she was with people.

Rose was very, very happy when she found that her parents would be returning to the states. Thanks to Mike, now they would have time to look for a more permanent home. Rose felt so grateful to both her parents for all the encouragement they had given her over the years, especially the last couple of years.

She thought about the upcoming visit of Martha and Bill. They sounded so nice on the phone. They must be feeling some angst about seeing their former son-in-law get married. Rose decided that if they did seem concerned she would do everything she could to make them comfortable.

And then there was Tim. Tim, who had grown up never having a mother in the home, and now when he is almost prepared to go on his own, there is suddenly a woman there. Before he left for school he seemed so happy and content. Would being away these months have changed him? She was surprised at how much she missed him - missed having him drop in - missed his witty remarks and his ability to make them laugh - missed seeing the close bond he had with his father.

Mike. Her Mike. She never thought that anyone could ever make her feel the way he did. It would be wonderful to look over in the bed each morning and see him there; to have him turn out the light and hold her close each night.

Whatever did I do to deserve such happiness, she wondered?

But it was time to get moving. Christmas trees in both houses were decorated and both refrigerators filled with food.

Christmas cards had been sent. It was amazing how quickly all the plans came together. Her friends had been so generous with their time to help her get everything done so she wouldn't get too tired.

Rose kept her eye on the clock. Soon Jeff called to say his grandparents had landed and they would soon be on their way to Nuna Lake. And finally Jenny called to say they would be there in half an hour. Rose began to get very excited. Mike was due to be at the house when they arrived. Would he make it? She began to watch out the window and then got her coat and went out on the porch. Even in the winter, the grounds of her property were colorful. The view of the lake stayed beautiful. She gave a sigh of relief when Mike pulled into the driveway, followed almost immediately by Jeff, Karen, Jenny, Ann and John. She ran to greet her parents.

At first she could not let go of either of them and then she spotted Mike, standing back and waiting. She reached out and pulled him close saying, "This is Mike." There were hugs and kisses and wonderful confusion. Jeff had already started inside with luggage and soon they all joined him.

They had time for a brief visit and a nice dinner. Then Mike and Rose left for the local airport to meet Tim, Martha, and Bill.

This time, it was Rose who stood back and let Mike greet his family. Tim was so happy to see his dad, but then he spotted Rose, shouted, "Rosie" and lifted her off the ground in a big bear hug. Taking her hand, he led her to his grandparents. "This is Rosie. This is my grandpa and grandma."

They each gave Rose a hug and thanked her for including them at this special time. On their way home they stopped at Rose's so the two families could meet. Jeff and Tim immediately isolated themselves in a corner for guy talk. But because it was getting late Mike hurried them on their way so everyone could get rested for the big day tomorrow.

Chapter 17

Rose felt wonderful when she woke up on her wedding day. She felt like shouting for everyone to hear, "Gooooood Morning, America! This *is* the first day of the rest of *my* life!" I wonder if I should write to that station and let them know how important that phrase has been to me, she thought. It might even be a recorded announcement. No matter. She got the message.

She made her way downstairs very quietly and quickly, grabbed her jacket and headed into the woods. The earth underneath her feet was covered with frost and sounded crunchy as she walked into the woods in the clear, crisp air. For just a few minutes on this frosty morning she wanted to sit on her bench. She sat there, quietly meditating on her new life. She began to pray, thanking the Lord for leading her on a new pathway. If Rob had not left her she might have continued existing, not living life so fully. She wondered if she would have had the courage to leave him if she had known he had another love. Probably not, she thought. I would just have tried harder to be what I thought he wanted me to be. Rob would have pushed me away if I had still been with him when

I found out I had cancer. As hard as it had been at first, today she was so happy. Mike is so good to me, she thought. Always encouraging me. Taking care of me. She was thankful for so many things.

When she got back to the house she started to prepare breakfast. Certainly there had to be blueberry pancakes, bacon and sausage and eggs. As the aroma of the bacon filled the house, the family found their way downstairs. Everyone was in a happy mood as they ate and shared family stories. Jeff wanted to take John on a quick canoe ride to show him the lake and the new special cove he and Karen, and Jenny had found. Jenny and Karen decided to run into town to see the Christmas celebration at Sarah's. Rose sent them on their way. As they cleaned up after the meal, Rose and her mother at last had time to have a quiet mother/daughter talk.

"Did you ever think I'd meet someone like Mike," Rose asked her mother.

"I had no way of knowing for sure but I hoped you would. Rose, I was blest twice with two good men. Your father was so protective of me, wanting me to have the best. Not material things, but encouraging people who would build me up, not make me doubt myself. When he died I thought my world would end. But I had you. Even as a little girl you seemed to sense my moods. I would be feeling sad and you would bring your doll to me because it needed its grandma. Or you would reach out and take my hand. I knew I needed to be strong for you. I thought I could never love anyone again. It was very natural for John and I to reach out for each other after Ruth died. I found that I could love again as John and I spent more time together. As positive as I am that it was the right step for me to take, I know this is also the right step for you to take. John and I are so happy for you," she said giving her daughter a hug.

"I'm so very happy you and John will be living so close by.

I know we don't have much time to visit today," Rose began, "but we'll have lots of time later."

Jenny and Karen came back and reported that Sarah's shop was filled with people. They laughed as they told about Will in a big black top hat and red jacket greeting people and opening the doors. "I bet Nuna Lake will never forget this day," Karen said.

Finally, at last, it was time to get ready. The girls gave Rose a manicure and a pedicure and helped her with her hair.

Mike had insisted he would drive Rose to the chapel. "We're not kids," he told her. "I want to walk in the door holding your hand so you won't change your mind." Nothing would dissuade him from his plan.

Rose waited anxiously for him to arrive. She opened the door as soon as she heard the car pull in the driveway. He stepped back in amazement for a second.

"Wow," he said as he wrapped his arms around her. "I have never seen anyone so beautiful."

"Hey, Mike, do we pass inspection?" Jenny playfully asked.

Mike gave Jenny and Karen a one-armed hug while holding onto Rose with the other.

"I can't believe how beautiful you all are."

"Hey, Tim, my feelings are hurt. Your dad didn't tell us we're beautiful, too," Jeff teased.

"I noticed that. I even took a shower and put a suit on. Oh, well, I guess we know how we rate in his life," Tim answered. Then looking out the door, Tim said, "I think we can go now."

With Rose and Mike leading the way the family followed them down off the porch.

"What's this?" Mike called out. A long stretch limo was waiting to take them all to the church. "Who arranged this?"

"It was Jeff," Tim said. And Jeff added, "It was really grandpa's idea. But I thought it was a good one."

Then Mike said, "Let's go, everybody. I can't wait any longer to be married."

The chapel was located inside the church just around the corner from the main sanctuary. Tim stepped ahead of them to open the doors.

Rose stopped. She looked back at Mike and then back inside the chapel. It was filled with red roses. White ribbons had been placed along the short aisle with a red rose tucked in the bow. Red roses were lining the altar and on the windowsills. White candles were flickering above them. Soft music was playing in the background. The minister in his white robe was waiting for them.

"Oh, Mike, oh Mike." she kept repeating.

"You said you wanted to be married in the rose garden. This was the closest I could make it happen in December."

With the parents sitting in the pews and Tim, Jeff, Jenny, and Karen, standing by their sides, Rose and Mike repeated their vows, and exchanged two plain gold bands, and pledged their love to each other forever. As the minister neared the end of the service, he asked for Ann, John, Martha and Bill to come forward. Then he asked the eight of them to form a circle around the couple as he gave the final blessing. "May you always be surrounded with love," he told them.

"Now it's time for food," Tim told them as they walked out the door. The driver congratulated them as they entered the limo and asked if they wanted to make any stops before going to the restaurant. They decided to go directly there.

As they approached the Lake House they could see the parking lot filled with cars.

"This must be a very big party they're having tonight," Rose said. She had already explained that they would be in a small room in the back.

With Rose and Mike leading the way, the family made their way from the limo to the entrance. They could hear music from a band.

As they opened the door the music stopped suddenly and then they heard the band begin to play *Here Comes the Bride*!

Rose looked at Mike and asked, "What is this?" Mike looked very puzzled as he said, "I have absolutely *no* idea."

Their family gently pushed them inside the restaurant amid much cheering and clapping.

Neither Mike nor Rose could really understand what was happening. The entire restaurant had been turned into a rose garden. There were bouquets of roses of all colors on every table and rose bushes along the walls among some green ferns and small palm trees. There was an archway decorated with roses with a bench underneath, much like the bench in Rose's garden, so they could sit and greet their guests. Outside the picture windows and the door walls of the restaurant, twinkling lights had been placed along the shoreline. It looked magical.

Mike was really stunned. He looked really surprised. "Did you arrange this?" he asked Rose. "Absolutely not. Be honest, Mike, did you do this?"

"I did not," he said. "There is only one person I know who could have pulled this off. We must have every rose in this part of the country. It had to be Gabe." Gabe was his general manager.

The mayor came to the microphone and asked for everyone's attention. "When we heard that two of our favorite people were getting married, the town wondered what we could do to make the day special for you both. Mike, the gardens you designed, and Rose, the gardens you chose for your property, have put Nuna Lake on the map. You both do so much for our town we want to say thank you to each of you. We want to share in this special day. This party is for you."

Mike kept shaking his head back and forth as he and Rose were gently pushed to the microphone. "How did this town ever keep a secret of this size? And this place. It is really beautiful. Gabe, I know you must have had a hand in getting so many roses. Are there any left in the eastern states?" Laughing,

Gabe shook his head no. Mike then went on, "Thank you so very, very much. I guess I'm pretty speechless right now." He handed the microphone to Rose.

"You are the dearest, sweetest people in the world. I can't believe what you have done for us. We are so happy to have you all here to share this day with us. I can't believe how many of you were willing to give up a Saturday night to be here. And you did it so quickly."

"Yes, that's right. We're just good," a voice from the crowd called out and made everyone laugh.

Then a voice sounding a bit like Tim's came out of the crowd. "Enough speeches. Let's party."

The band began to play. Some people began to dance, some to eat, and some came to Rose and Mike to offer congratulations. Will and Sarah waved to them from the dance floor. Julia and her husband were there. They saw Tim dancing with Katy. Rose's friends from the shelter group were there with their husbands. All of Mike's staff at the firm was there with their spouses as well as most of the town. Don and Beth Cunningham offered congratulations.

Harry and Millie were among the first to officially greet them. "Oh, Millie, it is so wonderful for you to come. I am so glad you can be here," Rose told her giving her a hug.

"Rose, my Harry told me he would bring me in a wheelchair if I needed it. I did so want to see you. You look beautiful because you're happy."

As Gabe and his wife came by, Mike asked him how he managed to get so many roses at this time of the year. Gabe told him it took a lot of phone calls but it was well worth it.

"Gabe, I can't even imagine how much work and time it took for you to change a dining room into a garden." Mike added, "You know, I don't believe I have ever stopped to look at the beauty of the roses. I have seen them as part of a bigger plan, checking the setting and the sunlight and....well, more botanical things. This setting is magnificent. How can I ever thank you for making it happen?" Rose added, "I didn't know roses came in so many different colors."

"Well, Mike and Rose, it all started when someone in town wanted to know what to buy you two as a wedding gift. Pots and pans didn't seem to be the answer. Rose had mentioned that if summer had not been so far off she would have invited everyone and get married in her rose garden. Mike, practically everyone in town has a garden you created. So we decided to give you a garden on your special day."

Guests came and went during the evening. It felt as if Rose or Mike was a personal friend to everyone. After greeting guests from the arbor, they started to mingle among the crowd. When Rose finally made her way to her family, she asked them if they had known about this wonderful surprise. "Oh, yes," they told her.

"Jenny, I didn't think you could keep a secret that well," Rose told her daughter. "It was hard," she told her mom. "Especially when you kept changing the menu for our dinner."

As the evening drew to a close and guests started to leave, Tim brought his dad's car to the door. Mike and Rose planned to drive to a cabin in the woods. They would return home on Christmas morning.

Rose and Mike turned to each member of their family. Rose reached out and took the hands of Martha and Bill. "Mike has told me how much you have done for him, keeping him going during the rough days. I want you to know you will always, always be a part of our family. I hope we can talk on the phone and visit each other."

"We're happy that Mike has someone to share his life with." Martha told her. "We thought it should have happened years ago, but now we're happy he waited for you." Bill added.

Rose turned to her mother and John. "You have been with me through so many things in my life. How could I ever, ever thank you for keeping me sane during the past couple of years?"

"By being happy." they told her. "We're happy for you, Rose. Enjoy each day. Treasure each moment you have together."

The four young people stood side by side. As they gave each one a hug, each one of them gave Rose and Mike some advice as they got into the car.

At last, Mike and Rose drove away from the Lake House. They looked at each other and smiled. They realized they were not driving away......they were driving forward. They were driving toward their future.